Beyond Bonds Nirmohi & Other Short Stories

Dr. Abhinandan Ballary, D.Litt

TANEESHA PUBLISHERS

Title   :   Beyond Bonds Nirmohi & Other Short Stories

Author :   Dr. Abhinandan Ballary, D.Litt

Edition :   First (August, 2024)

ISBN   :   9788197792717

Published by

TANEESHA PUBLISHERS | *A Venture by -* **PRACHI DIGITAL PUBLICATION**

Regd. Add.: 254, Khuriyakhatta No. 10, Bindukhatta,
Lalkuan, Nainital - 262402, Uttarakhand, India
Website : www.taneeshapublishers.in
E-mail : taneeshapublishers@gmail.com
Phone : +91 845481 2712, +91 976041 7980

Printed by :

Manipal Technologies Limited, Bengaluru - 560001, Karnataka

INDEX

Preface

Dear Reader,

I am thrilled to present to you "Nirmohi & Other Short Stories." Each story in this collection has been crafted with care, drawing inspiration from everyday life and the extraordinary moments hidden within it. Through these narratives, I aim to explore the depths of human emotions and the complexities of relationships.

As you turn the pages, you will encounter characters facing a variety of situations—some heartwarming, some challenging, but all profoundly human. These stories are meant to provoke thought, evoke emotion, and perhaps even inspire you to see your own life from a new perspective.

What secrets will be uncovered? What lessons will be learned? I invite you to dive into these tales and find out. I hope you enjoy reading them as much as I enjoyed writing them.

Happy reading!

Warm regards,

Dr. Abhinandan Ballary, D.Litt

Author

Neelu

Every day, near the Parijata tree in our backyard, I would find myself watching her. There was something about her gentle smile that caught me. As time passed, I didn't even realize how much I started to admire her. I didn't know much about her, but somehow, she had found a special place in my heart. On one particularly hot afternoon, while I was lost in thoughts about her, my mother's voice suddenly broke through, "Prem, come see who's here," she called out. I was a bit annoyed to be pulled away from my daydreams but went anyway, only to see my dad and uncle waiting. My uncle, with a warm smile, patted my back and said, "You're doing great, Prem." I just nodded and said, "Hmm, uncle." Then he mentioned, "Prem, Sariyu was asking about you," but I didn't really react. However, he seemed happy to tell me, "She sent you rasgullas because she knows you like them." Again, I just hummed in response. My short answers and lack of attention seemed to bother my dad, who scolded me, "You need to talk properly... they've come a long way... don't just hum." Pretending to be confused, I asked, "What are you talking about, dad?" He lost his patience and said, "Acting like you don't know... we're talking about your marriage. They can't wait forever."

Feeling brave all of a sudden, as if the girl I saw by the Parijata tree gave me courage, I spoke my mind. "Why should anyone wait for me? Sariyu can surely find someone better. It would be right to find her someone else, uncle," I found myself saying, surprising even me. My uncle Srinivas, caught off guard by what I said, looked at my dad, confused. "What's this all of a sudden? You were quiet, and now you're saying all this," he said, clearly shocked. My mom, who had been listening from the kitchen, joined in with both worry and firmness. "What's going on, Prem? Why cause a fuss now? Sariyu is wonderful and right for you. She really likes you. Weren't you the one who wanted to wait until you finished your studies and got a job?" she reminded me kindly but firmly.

Then, my mom made up her mind and said to Uncle Srinivas, "We should start getting things ready," clearly stating she was making the decision for me. Her voice was calm but had a final tone to it. Uncle Srinivas, now with the job of making arrangements, looked at me kindly but sadly. "Only God knows what's going on in your heart, Prem. Perhaps we're moving too fast. Let's keep hope," he said, his voice full of regret. Hearing him made me feel guilty, stirring up a lot of thoughts I didn't say out loud. "Why do they get to decide my future like my feelings don't matter?" I wondered quietly to myself as I walked away, leaving the heavy mood and the big decisions being made without me behind.

On that memorable day, under the gentle shade of the Parijata tree in backyard of our garden, my mother was deep in conversation with her, a woman whose voice was rumored to be so melodious, it could make even the cuckoo jealous. This was not just any visitor; she was someone whose elegance and charm were often the subject of many conversations within our family circle, yet I had never personally witnessed her allure until that moment.

As I stealthily approached, drawn by the intrigue and the snippets of praise I had overheard, I remained unseen, a silent observer to this meeting. The sunlight danced through the leaves, illuminating her in a soft glow that seemed almost divine, accentuating her presence against the backdrop of our tranquil garden. My curiosity was not just piqued by the tales of her enchanting voice but also by the mystery that seemed to surround her.

Then, as if sensing an audience, she turned swiftly, her eyes meeting mine with an expression of surprise that momentarily disrupted the calm of the scene, much like a pebble disturbing the surface of a still pond. My eyes, betraying my intrigue, drifted to the Mangalsutra resting against her chest, a stark reminder of her marital status, which sent a jolt of reality through me. The sight of the ring on her toe anchored that reality further. My unwavering gaze, perhaps too intense, caused a blush to spread across her beautiful face, adding an unintended charm to the moment.

"I'm going inside," she hastily told my mother, her voice carrying a mix of embarrassment and urgency, as she moved away like a startled deer, oblivious to my mother's attempts to halt her departure with calls of "Hey Neela, Neelaanjane, stop." The name "Neelaanjane" lingered in the air, a name as exquisite as the bearer herself, but tinged with the bittersweet realization of her unattainability. My dreams, so vivid moments before, now lay fragmented by the harsh truth of her marital commitment. How merciless the truth can be, revealing the futility of my newfound affection. Yet, how does one quell a heart that has found a sincere admiration? How can societal norms dictate the matters of the heart? My thoughts grew heavy with these reflections.

"Is it possible to fall so deeply with merely a few glimpses? You must forget her," I admonished myself, knowing all too well the pain that such unrequited feelings could bring. "Such sentimentality only leads to sorrow. Be wary! Yes, you must forget her. But how?" The dilemma of a sentimental fool, caught between the sorrow of unfulfilled desires and the inexplicable joy they bring. Despite the turmoil, I resolved not to seek her out the following morning, yet as dawn broke, my resolve waned, and my heart yearned once more for a sight of her. Drawn irresistibly to the door, there she stood under the Parijata tree, adorned in a celestial cascade of white and red flowers that seemed to shower her in divine beauty.

My fascination with her beauty deepened with each passing day. During this time, my uncle made another visit. He showed remarkable patience with my absent-mindedness. Due to my job, I had to undertake a six-month training program in a different location, which meant leaving behind Neelaanjane, the one whose beauty had become the essence of my existence. Throughout my time away, there wasn't a single day I didn't find myself thinking of her. Returning home turned out to be a heart-wrenching experience. The dreams and feelings I harbored dissipated as if they were mere bubbles on the surface of water. The allure of her beauty lost its grip on me, and what was once adoration morphed into a source of anguish. A profound emptiness took hold, making every experience seem fleeting and temporary. In my sorrow, I found solace in reading about the life of the first Tirthankara, Purudeva. In the grand court of Indra, where music and dance reigned supreme, the story tells of Neelaanjane's breathtaking performance that enchanted all, including King Purudeva himself, who was bewitched by her grace and beauty, deeming it a timeless truth. Yet, fate intervened, and Neelaanjane's life was abruptly cut short mid-performance, leaving nothing but her memory behind. Indra, fearing the loss of joy her absence would bring and the crumbling of the illusion he had so carefully constructed, used his divine powers to create a semblance of Neelaanjane to continue the dance. This deception was executed with such finesse that it went unnoticed by all but Purudeva, who was struck by the realization of life's transient nature. The Neelaanjane he had known and adored was gone forever. The stark realization of this impermanence, witnessing the dissolution of what seemed an eternal verity, instilled in him a sense of detachment. As onlookers remained engrossed, he withdrew, embracing the notion that all he had experienced was nothing but a dream.

"What happened to Neelaanjane?" My voice carried the weight of sudden anxiety when I learned she had been hospitalized. My mother's reply was laden with a deep sadness, "She was always so radiant, a true princess. It's hard to say how long that illness was silently spreading within her..." The gravity of her words echoed in my heart, amplifying my concern. "Leprosy," she disclosed somberly, and that revelation struck me with the force of a thunderclap, demolishing the sanctified place in my heart where I had enshrined Neelaanjane, reducing it to ashes. The depth of my affection for her beauty, which I had naively believed to be eternal, now seemed a distant dream. Was her unmatched grace merely a fleeting gift, destined to be cruelly snatched away? How could destiny be so merciless as to mar such purity with the scourge of disease? The inexorable decrees of fate, it appeared, spared no one. Amidst the whirlwind of my thoughts, a quiet prayer for her swift recovery emerged as a beacon of hope.

"Prem," my mother's call snapped me back to reality, pulling me from the depths of my reflections. My uncle was there, anticipation etched across his face. "What's your decision, Prem?" he inquired, his voice tinged with a mixture of hope and urgency. The thought of adding to their burdens felt utterly wrong. With a sense of resignation, I acquiesced to their wishes. Their faces lit up with unbridled joy at my consent. "Vishalu, your son has consented... By God's grace, I'll not trouble you further. We must now make arrangements for the wedding," they exclaimed, their relief and happiness palpable. As my mother beckoned Srinivas to serve coffee, my uncle, buoyed by the news, began to stride away triumphantly, his steps lively. He brandished his umbrella with the flair of a man who had conquered formidable challenges, moving with the confidence of one who had vanquished foes in three realms. Witnessing their elation, I stood rooted to the spot, speechless, my heart torn between the harsh realities of life's afflictions and the genuine warmth of familial joy.

Sukanya

It is said that even if one organ of an extraordinary person is impaired, God grants them unparalleled strength in another. Similarly, our story's hero, despite losing the ability to see the light of life, has gained a melodious voice and the ability to sing beautifully. Surprisingly, to those who see him, he doesn't appear blind. There is a certain light in his blind eyes... one eye even has a peculiar gleam. There he stands, waiting for his wife. He cannot see anything. His wife must come to guide him, but where has she gone? Crossing the big road to drop the children at the school on the other side takes at least half an hour. After that, she comes to him and takes him to the music school where he gives music lessons. When she returns, one of the students helps him get home. This has been the routine for the past four or five years. She has become a symbol of immense patience. This unique life has taught her many things. Despite being married to a blind man, she smiles.

He sits in a porch-like space adjacent to the shop. When bored, he stands up, leans against the porch, and sings softly. Sometimes, lost in the music, his voice gets louder. A tuft of his curly hair sways over his forehead. A faint smile, almost invisible, spreads across his face. His body seems a bit emaciated. Perhaps to bring some stability, he seems to make a futile effort by putting his hand in his pant pocket, or it might be his habit since childhood. Look, here comes Sukanya. Sorry, I haven't introduced her to you... no, she will introduce herself.

"I am Sukanya, a girl from a middle-class family. I don't have parents. My brothers are everything to me. I may not be very beautiful, but I am decent enough. As youth has taken over my body, there's a certain glow to it. Among my three brothers, the eldest is a bit hot-tempered, but he's close to my heart. I am studying for a B.A. degree at a college. After my brother got transferred from Mangalore to here, I enrolled for my degree at the local college. I scored well in my PUC, so I got a seat quickly, and it's been only four or five days since college started. On my way from home to the bus stop, I noticed a man staring at me intensely near the shop at the turn. One day, I heard him singing softly while looking at me, and I got scared. I thought of changing my route, but the other way is also crowded. At first, I didn't pay much attention.

The man's face looked kind, but gradually his sweet voice, in some way, started to captivate my heart. Without realizing it, I was drawn to him. He isn't exceptionally handsome... but the indescribable expression on his face and his singing drew me in. I always loved good songs, and it became impossible to pass by the shop without looking at him. No matter how much I told myself not to care, unknowingly, he started to make a place in my heart. I wanted to push back that lock of curly hair on his forehead with my hand once. His well-built body and the way he stood with his hand in his pocket became endearing to me. Poor guy! He looks at me every day but never behaves rudely. This is the nature of love! Once trapped in it, it's over! Sukanya has fallen into the trap of such love."

Now I will continue the story. Sukanya mentally prepared herself to tell her elder brother about the charming singer, wondering how to express her feelings and in what words. One day, she slowly sat down and told him. Her brother's reaction was not as encouraging as she had hoped! "Sukanya, your love is strange. Falling in love without knowing who, what, and how they are? This is a world of deceit," he said. She replied, "I don't know, brother, but he seems like a good person. Talk to him once."

The next day, as Sukanya hurried to college, she froze at the sight in front of her. Before she could close her eyes, she saw her brothers beating him mercilessly, and he lay on the ground. Blood started to flow from his forehead, hands, and legs. They were cursing him with harsh words and beating him ruthlessly. "Girls shouldn't be walking alone... you scoundrel... you dare to sing... what a menace," said the shopkeeper. "Stop, sir, how much more will you hit him... he can't see, he's blind..." But they didn't care to listen. Sukanya heard everything. She immediately stood in between and said, "Brother, stop, please don't hit him." She wiped the blood from his head with her saree. He was unconscious. "Brother, stop. If he dies, you will all end up in jail. First, arrange to take him to the hospital," she said. By then, his wife had arrived and was shocked by the sight. "Oh my God! What is this? What happened?" she screamed, becoming speechless upon seeing her husband's condition. Sukanya asked, "Who are you?" The shopkeeper, taken aback, said, "She is his wife, Kanamma... without seeing or knowing anything, your brothers caught and beat him. Poor woman... she brings her blind husband here every day...." The woman fell weeping at her husband's feet. Sukanya stood there, speechless. They immediately took both of them to the hospital.

Time carries countless events within its womb and moves forward. Three years have passed since this incident. Now, Sukanya doesn't need to drop the children at school; her husband himself drops them off and then goes to the music school. He now sees the light of the world through Sukanya's eyes, which he has made his own... It was Sukanya's last wish, who passed away in a road accident a year ago: "To donate her eyes to the musician."

Maya

Maya sat in front of the mirror, feeling very disillusioned. Getting ready, which used to be fun, now felt like a "performance drama." Her long black hair, which she once loved, lay on her back, showing how unhappy she was. She muttered to herself, "Which so-called perfect husband is it today? His family will come, inspect me like I'm livestock—checking my eyes, my legs, maybe even asking me to sing. Then there's the feast my mom prepared: the upma with vegetables, the kesari bath dripping with ghee, and the Chikmagalur filter coffee. But in a few days, they'll probably find some reason to reject me." She knew this was often because of dowry demands.

Trying to push away her frustration, Maya thought, "I'm not unattractive. I have a decent height, a dusky complexion, and my black eyes are nice, as my friends often say without jealousy." My family sent my younger sister, who is prettier than me, to our grandmother's house in the village. Some men saw her and thought she might be a good match. My father insisted my younger sister wouldn't get married until I did, setting a strict rule. So, she stayed at our grandmother's house whenever potential grooms came. I was the one they examined. But I wasn't interested; maybe if I were a rich man's daughter, I'd have a chance. This one makes the twelfth. Let's see if this one is any different. As my mother Vaishali called out, 'What happened, Maya? It's time for them to arrive. Get ready quickly,' I felt annoyed. 'Go, Ma, I'm tired. I don't feel like dressing up anymore,' I replied. But my mother comforted me. 'Be patient, my daughter. It's been a long time. Just wait for this one. The matchmaker said he's a simple, good man,' she said. I laughed sarcastically, 'Which man didn't the matchmaker praise? He says the same thing about everyone.' Not wanting to upset my mother, I got ready quickly.

The groom's family sat in the living room. The smell of vegetable-spiced upma filled the air. Maya came in with plates and served them. The groom looked slightly plump, ordinary-looking, and somewhat dark-skinned, with a serious expression and a small smile.

"Does it even matter anymore? Whether this is attempt number twelve or thirteen?" she thought, not caring about the outcome. Most of the families that rejected her did so for money, while some said, "She's okay, but it would be better if she had a job." "Let's see what this so-called prince thinks," she thought, knowing the groom's family usually made the decision. After several days of silence, she felt the familiar sting of rejection—a feeling she was used to. "This rejection cycle is a never-ending routine," she reflected. "It's time I told my parents to stop trying." Her mother, Vishalakshamma, made the best upma, and neighbors often praised it, saying, "If it's masala upma, Vaishali's is the best."

After many rejections, Maya started thinking about a life without marriage. She spent her time tailoring, finding comfort in her work, especially in saree fall stitching. She saved money and took typing courses, inspired by friends who got jobs through computer courses. The silence from the groom's family, while sad for her parents, made her more determined to follow her own path.

Maya often went to the library near her house to get good novels. Reading helped her relax and forget her problems for a while. It was refreshing to get lost in stories, sometimes with her sister or her brother's kids joining her. One day, she took some storybooks to the park next to the library where her brother's children were playing happily. Her brother had moved to a new place a year ago because his wife wanted to, but his kids still loved spending time with Maya.

While reading, she suddenly looked up and saw the twelfth man she was supposed to meet after they saw each other the previous week. Seeing him unexpectedly made her face turn red with embarrassment. "Surprised to see me?" he asked. Maya was flustered and could only say, "Ah... no... no..."

He sat next to her on the bench and said, "I was supposed to come to your house, Maya. But finding you here makes it easier to talk. I'll just ask you straight. If you think we could get along, tell me." Hearing him speak so directly made Maya feel excited and nervous.

Hearing his words, Maya felt a rush of excitement. He was the first man to give her a real chance. She wondered if this was real and pinched herself to make sure. He continued, "I might not look like a hero from the stories, and I'm not very tall. I have a simple job, but I think we can have a good life together. You seem to agree," he said, making her name sound the sweetest it ever had. Then he gently urged, "Don't be shy, can you look at me?"

Maya bravely met his gaze. This time, her smile was real, filled with warmth and affection, unlike the forced ones before. Looking into his eyes, she felt surrounded by care and love. "I'll always be there for you," he promised her. But Maya had to ask, "Do your family members feel the same way? We can't meet a big dowry demand."

He replied, "I'm the one marrying you. It's enough that we do what's right for your family. My family isn't after money. They value what I want. But enough about me. What do you think? Are you okay with me?"

Maya, blushing shyly, admitted, "Your kindness has already won me over." In her mind, she saw him not just for his looks but for his character, thinking of him as a person mighty in spirit if not in stature.

Revelation

Harsha was lost in his thoughts in the gentle caress of Kavya. Outside, the thunder of the rain and the constant crackle of lightning could be heard. Kavya, with half-closed eyes, was staring out of the window bars as if in anticipation of someone. The occasional lightning in the sky captivated her. Wasn't it on a similar rainy night that Harsha was introduced, and within a few days, it turned into love, marriage, and now, she was living with the explosive secret, the cataclysmic truth that had emerged just a few days ago?

Born into a loving family, she had been well taught by her parents what love, affection, and care meant. They had instilled in her the values of not hurting others and to stand up against injustice and correct it if possible. Whatever Harsha had hidden from her, the truth she was unaware of, she had come to know just a few days ago. How did her heart endure that harsh truth! Now, just like the torrential rain outside, her heart was crying. Anger was also boiling up inside her.... But in life, many situations have to be handled with patience and wisdom....

Kavya came out of her thoughts. Harsha was holding her hands and saying something, "Kavi.... Do you remember.... Wasn't it on a night like this, with the rain pouring, that I first saw you? How pleasant was that night, remember?" "Yes!" she replied absentmindedly. Harsha sat up properly, "Why, dear, are you upset with me?" Without revealing her mind, she said, "Oh no, why would I be upset with you?" and turned her gaze outside again. The rain was getting heavier by the minute... the electric light was flickering.

Suddenly, she remembered. "Oh no," Kavya exclaimed as she ran to the kitchen. "Oh no, it's leaking so much. No matter how many times I tell him to change the house, he never listens," she said as she placed a vessel under the leaky roof and went out. Seeing that Kavya was still distracted even after speaking to her a second time, Harsha said, "Never mind, forget it," and turned on the TV.

A scene from Kuvempu's 'Varsha Bhairava' song was playing on the TV. "The stolen days of darkness, a rainy night, lightning quivers, the mountain, the forested earth, the golden creeper, as if sprouting from the clouds...."

"Kavya, today I'll arrange the food on the dining table. Come, let's eat," said Harsha.

Kavya replied, "No, Harsha, wait a while. I'm not hungry right now."

To this, he responded, "Alright then... as you wish," and headed to the kitchen. Returning, he relaxed on the sofa, listening to the TV. The last line of the 'Varsha Bhairava' song struck him: "This is not rain, this is the fervor of a deluge."

Kavya was lost in her thoughts, "Why haven't they arrived yet? What could happen to Harsha when they do? What kind of deluge might occur in his heart? Will he resort to another chain of lies to convince me? But I won't fall into that web of lies again."

Yet, Harsha is her husband, and her tender heart couldn't bear to treat him harshly. What could she do? Just as the poet described, 'The sky has turned into water, pouring down incessantly,' the rain was pouring down like a mad frenzy. Would the rain stop for a while, so it wouldn't be difficult for them to arrive? Kavya wondered.

The light in front of the house illuminated a small distance. She noticed two figures walking towards their cottage. Her heart started beating rapidly. They had arrived. Looking at Harsha, he was comfortably lounging on the sofa, engrossed in the TV. As soon as the doorbell rang, Kavya quickly ran and opened the door. A woman, drenched and shivering in her wet sari, holding the hand of a little girl, entered the house.

"Please come in... your name is Harini, isn't it?" Kavya welcomed them.

Hearing the name 'Harini' from somewhere, Harsha, who was watching TV, was startled. Was this a dream? Who are these people, Kavya? He got up and came over. As soon as he saw the newcomers, he turned pale.

"Who are you? Why are you here? Kavya, do you open the door for just anyone? It's dangerous. Why would you open the door on such a night?"

Kavya's voice turned stern, "Just anyone, you say. Look properly.... yes, in a way, it's true.... she met you before I did.... Look properly.... the one you trampled under your feet, the one who lost her hopes.... the dark circles under her eyes tell the tale.... her cheeks are sunken.... and look there, that little girl! She is your very own!"

Harsha, gathering all his strength, shouted, "Kavya!"

Kavya thundered back, "Why are you screaming as if you're going to lose your refuge? Don't you have the courage to face the truth? It's surprising to see such harsh truths hidden behind your innocent face."

Kavya's face was red with anger, and Harsha, unable to withstand her fiery gaze, felt defeated. Kavya's rage had not subsided. ""After seeing another beautiful girl, will you also leave me like you left

Harini? How do you deceive innocent women, Harsha?"

"Please, Kavya, stop. I did wrong, it's true, but I'm not so cunning as to deceive you. I hid it because I feared losing you if you found out I was married. Fifteen days ago, I heard about the floods in Gangapur that washed away the entire village. I was distressed, worrying about Harini and the child...."

Kavya interrupted, "What use is mere pity and compassion if not translated into action? You made sure I never received any of Harini's letters, in which she longed for you. It was only by chance that one letter, written after she survived the flood with the help of some kind souls, reached me. Otherwise, Harini would never have come to us...."

Harini started crying, and her words came out in between sobs, "When he drove me out of the house, I was a mother to a tiny baby. It was raining heavily, just like now...." She paused, her crying overwhelming her speech. Kavya placed a comforting hand on her shoulder. Harini continued, "A few days ago, floods in Gangapur washed away everything. Many lost their homes. Some compassionate person saved us both."

Harsha, unable to bear it, rushed to Harini, "Forgive me, Harini, I have wronged you greatly."

Kavya's voice was stern, "In these five years, you haven't understood my nature, Harsha? Do you think I want to build my life's dream palace on the grave of another woman's happiness? Harini is like a village flower. It's not enough to just say you wronged her; you must rectify her life. Come, sister, you have a right to live in this house. Let's live together. My parents didn't raise me to lose humanity." She then affectionately embraced the little girl. "The same rain that separated us has now witnessed our reunion," she said, smiling.

Harsha and Harini stood speechless. Tears flowed from Harini's eyes like the incessant rain outside. She ran and embraced Kavya, "You are so good!" she said in a choked voice, kissing Kavya's hands with affection. Kavya wiped her tears and said, "Why shed more tears now?" "These are tears of joy," Harini replied.

Harsha sighed deeply, as if a heavy burden had been lifted from his chest. The rain continued to pour, as if silently witnessing countless reunions, separations, joys, and sorrows. "The sky has turned into water, pouring down incessantly...."

Destiny's Canvas

One day, the painter was so disturbed that he wanted to throw away all the paintings he had hung around the room, the colors scattered here and there, and the brushes, never to be seen by his eyes again... far, far away.

Yes! It was his wife's harsh words that prompted him to do this act. "Playing with colors and brushes and sitting and painting all the time, does that fill our stomachs? It should remain a hobby, not a means of livelihood... My father warned me... but I didn't listen... Maybe I got enamored by your pretty face? You keep painting, and my children and I will starve! First, find a proper job with the degree you have. If you don't throw all these things away yourself, I will have to do it... Winning this contest, winning that contest... Promising millions, showing castles in the air... None of it has materialized. You take them to exhibitions, display them there, and then bring them back and hang them here... It's the same story! To take them and bring them back, we need to pay for auto-rickshaw fares!" she said angrily. Unable to bear it, he shouted back, "What is this, Madhu... why are you speaking so harshly? Is there a dagger in your heart? Don't you have any compassion? I have self-confidence, Madhu, one day I will surely win... Have patience." But despite his words, a cloud of despair darkened his face.

"Yes! Yes! You will win, and millions will come, so we have to sit and wait with our mouths open! By the time you win, our story will be over!" she said in discontent. Turning his face away in pain, he muttered, "What is this, Madhu... you are so furious today. You must have patience." She responded, "I don't know about all that. Within a month, you need to arrange for a lakh rupees for our son's engineering seat... otherwise, he will end up like you, a painter, and his wife and children will have to suffer the same way." Crying bitterly, she grabbed a canvas and tore it in anger. That furious act seemed to hurt him as if she had torn him. To him, everything that helped bring life to an empty canvas was not just objects; they were instruments of worship.

Is it as easy as she says? These are my life, he thought, gently stroking the torn canvas as if to soothe it. "Not today, but good days will come. How will she understand the joy of creating a painting? The ecstasy it brings when I am lost in it, forgetting the world's troubles as I draw each line! What does she know about that? Today, competition has increased in every field. Even a single step behind means a massive defeat." Taking a break from his thoughts, he organized the scattered colors, mixing plates, canvases, and brushes neatly.

Even in such a desperate state, the painter found that he... "a model" had come to him. Who was he? A watchman standing near the gate of a grand building in Devangari Colony when the artist was walking by.

The artist took two steps past the building but stopped and came back. The middle-aged man attracted the artist like a magnet. That serious face, long nose, and eyes radiating brilliance but slightly faded due to worry. The expression of contemplation was an ornament on that face. For some reason, that soul seemed to be in pain. Why wouldn't it have the power to attract anyone who saw it? The face, with its natural beauty and the constant thoughtful expression, had created an extraordinary attraction. The artist stood gazing at it, transfixed. As he stared intently, he felt it resembled someone. "Oh! It's at the tip of my tongue, but I can't remember," he muttered. "Oh, yes! Right, right, it's Rabindranath Tagore. If I give this long face a Tagore-like hairstyle instead of the stubbly beard... Wow! He would make a perfect model."

Noticing that an unknown person was staring at him so intently, the watchman got flustered and anxious. "Sir, who are you? What do you want?" he asked nervously. The painter, waking up from his trance, said, "Sorry, don't worry. I want to talk to you. Here, take this card. Come to my house in the evening after your duty. My phone number is on it." The man asked, "What is the matter, Sir?" The painter reassured him, "Don't worry, not here, come home," and walked on. "There are many ways to do good deeds. One soul connects with another, binds, and inspires to work together. How different are the worlds of a painter and a watchman? The artist's mind was imprinted with that face as if it were etched there forever.

At six in the evening, the watchman arrived at the painter's house. The artist greeted him, "Come in, come in. Was it hard to find the house?" To which he replied, "I have roamed around this area quite a bit, sir, so it wasn't difficult." The artist's wife peeked from inside and wondered, "Who is this? I've never seen this face before," and then went inside. "Come, let's go to my room," the artist said, leading him upstairs. The man commented on the spaciousness of the house. Hearing his strong voice, the wife, who was inside, muttered, "What else if not spacious? If my father hadn't given us this house, we would have ended up on the footpath... all because of trusting this line-drawer," grumbling as she went, the artist interrupted, "Madhu, why are you grumbling again? Keep it to yourself. Make a cup of strong coffee for our guest," he said. She replied sarcastically, "Look, you brought just one liter of milk... not enough for this house," to which he said, "Enough... manage with what we have." She retorted, "As you say." The artist then reassured her, "I'll explain everything to you later. Just meeting him made me feel that something good will come out of this. He seems very virtuous, and he might feel bad if he hears this. Just make it quietly and bring it," and then he went upstairs again. By the time he returned, the watchman was examining the paintings hung on the large hall's walls with great interest. The artist didn't interrupt his observation. By the time he finished, the artist's wife had brought two cups of coffee on a small tray. The watchman turned to the artist and said, "Did you paint all these, sir? They seem so lifelike as if they might come alive. You have painted beautifully," he said, smiling. The artist's wife, unable to stay quiet, remarked, "What if you feel that way? The judges who give awards didn't think so. What can we do? It's our fate!" she said. He looked at her, bewildered. The artist intervened, "Let's leave such talk. Come here, have some coffee... please sit," he said. She continued to grumble as she left, "If they come alive, we will have to leave the house," she muttered to herself and went away. The artist, grateful for his wife's momentary compassion, saw that she had made a cup of coffee for him as well. The artist said to the watchman, "Thank you for appreciating my paintings. Do you have an interest in painting?" .The watchman laughed loudly, "Me? No, sir. I have no interest in anything except guarding. It's just that seeing these brings joy to my heart. God has blessed me with that!" he said. After a brief silence, the artist began, "Yesterday, when you were standing near the gate... the main gate... as I walked past that big building, you caught my attention. I walked ahead but felt drawn back to you by some force. Watching you, I was reminded of our great poet 'Rabindranath Tagore.' If we style your hair like his, you would look just like the poet...," he said, making the man happy. "Sir, you are flattering me. Where is that great poet, and where am I? If you saw me like that, it's my fortune. I know a little about him as I have studied up to SSC. Please go on,' he said, eagerly listening to the artist. "I have decided to use you as my model for a painting. I feel it will bring me fame and awards," the artist said, moved by his emotions. The watchman laughed, "Sir, are you joking? You say you want to paint someone like me... my life depends on this guarding job. I have a family, wife, and children," he said seriously. The artist, with a bit of authority in his voice, said, "You must agree," and then softened his tone, "Please," he pleaded. The man relented, "Alright, sir. But what time should I come? It gets late normally," he said. The artist replied, "Your shift is during the day, right? Just come at six in the evening like today. Initially, stay a bit longer. I will tell you later. If this painting comes out well by God's grace, it might attract global attention and earn thousands of rupees," he said. The watchman, surprised, widened his eyes and exclaimed, "Really!" But there was no greed in his eyes, only natural astonishment. His inner purity shone through his face, creating the resemblance to the poet. The artist, admiring his model, said, "If I win any awards, you will deserve half of the prize. I promise," he said passionately. The watchman replied, "That's your greatness, sir. I don't expect that. May it bring good fortune. I will come from tomorrow," he said, folding his hands and standing up. The artist, in turn, said, "If this painting opens the doors of fortune, it will be good for both of us," as the watchman left the house.

Though the question, "Is it right for a good artist to think about the prize money before even starting the painting?" arose in his mind, painting was not just a hobby for him. It was a means to drive away poverty from his life. Since he had accepted it as a profession, the concern for the money needed for living was inevitable. The artist began to weave dreams about the painting he hadn't yet started. Poor man! He seemed very good-natured. Thinking of his father, the artist recalled how he had always been an admirer of Tagore. Knowing more about the poet and his works felt like understanding his inner self. This would help him create a lively painting. He decided to do Tagore's portrait with utmost devotion and reverence. It required enough mental preparation. He dusted off his collection of Tagore's works like 'Gitanjali,' 'Gora,' and other writings, setting them aside to read. The lines from 'Gitanjali' were dear to him: "Where the mind is without fear and the head is held high... into that heaven of freedom... let my country awake." What a noble wish! No one else had shaped educational philosophy as beautifully as Tagore a great humanist. Running educational institutions while bearing all the financial responsibilities was something Tagore himself experienced, facing many financial crises. His wife, Mrinalini Devi, took care of the children at Shantiniketan. Reading about how many days of financial hardship made them worried, yet they persevered, he tried to understand the great soul.

The next day, the watchman came. The artist had bought wigs and other things needed for the poet's hairstyle. When he dressed the watchman in the poet's attire, he was amazed, "What, you look just like Tagore!" he said, preparing to sketch while laughing. The watchman said, "Don't joke, sir," but the artist said, "Don't think it's a joke. You must feel as if you are the poet. If that feeling reflects in your face and eyes, it will help me a lot," he said earnestly. The watchman replied seriously, "Alright, sir," and the contemplative expression spread across his face. That was the look the artist needed!

For eight days, the artist immersed himself in the world of colors, working with dedication and devotion, creating a masterpiece with the help of his model. On the ninth day, the large painting came to life beautifully. Despite the back pain from sitting for long periods during the painting sessions, the model cooperated with calm patience. Overwhelmed with excitement at the sight of the finished painting, the artist lifted his model and danced with joy. Even though his wife had no interest in art, she viewed the painting with interest, believing it would bring them good fortune. Their son, too, was amazed and his eyes widened. The wife, who usually grumbled, was struck silent in astonishment.

With two weeks remaining for the national art exhibition in Delhi, the artist began preparing to take the painting of Tagore and some of his other best works. The model bid him farewell with love. In Delhi, his paintings caught everyone's attention. There was still plenty of time for the international art festival in Berlin. What followed seemed like a beautiful dream for the artist. The magnificent artwork won first prize in Berlin, securing a cheque for three lakhs, a trophy, and a large bouquet of shimmering soft flowers. Holding these in both hands, the emotional artist first thought of the model... Carrying the praises and congratulations of many, he returned home with a sense of gratitude and his prized paintings.

After the judges' verdict and the awarding of prizes, people eagerly gathered to see the winning works. They kept returning to the large portrait of Tagore, captivated by the intricate lines of indescribable pain and contemplation that the artist had captured with extraordinary tranquility on the face. Words like "marvelous!" and "beautiful!" echoed.

Remembering those moments, the artist's eyes filled with tears of joy. Foreign newspapers praised the artist's incredible achievement and published photos of the painting.

The model waited near his house, knowing the artist would arrive soon. The artist's arrival brought joy to everyone. His children welcomed him at the airport with garlands.When the artist arrived, his wife warmly welcomed him inside and treated him to coffee and snacks, congratulating him in a sweet voice. Many congratulated him. Upon reaching home, the artist embraced the model and said, "Didn't I tell you? The first prize would surely come," speaking with a full heart. The model, releasing himself from the hug, said, "Your hard work has paid off, sir. I am very, very happy," and placed a sandal wood garland around his neck. To the artist's wife, a prize of three lakhs for one painting seemed unbelievable. Although she couldn't understand the quality and excellence of the painting, the three lakhs had temporarily silenced her grumbling. What troubled the artist's mind was the half of the prize money he had promised to the model. The model wasn't one to desire it, but if the artist didn't keep his promise, would God be pleased with him?

Two days later, with a bag of money, the artist set out for the model's house. At around ten in the morning, he entered the house with a smile. The model welcomed him with astonishment and joy. Had it been anyone else, they might have pestered him for the prize money, but the model seemed to have no such expectations. He treated the artist with delicious coffee and snacks. It was an ordinary rented house, with the ceiling, walls, and floor in a poor state. How else could a poor watchman's house be? The model, lacking any shrewdness needed to survive in today's world, was a proud man.

The model expressed his happiness at the artist's visit, saying, "It is a great joy that you have come to my humble home." At that moment, his son entered the house. The young man, though tall, looked undernourished but was polite and greeted the artist respectfully, "Uncle, congratulations on winning the prize." The artist asked, "What are you studying my boy?" The boy replied, "I finished my PUC and got a donation seat for MBBS after the CET process, but..." He paused. His father looked at him disapprovingly. The artist urged, "Go on." The boy continued, "But arranging the donation money is difficult. We have somehow managed to collect fifty thousand. My mother sold all her old jewelry. Father just keeps worrying. He doesn't like to ask anyone for help, believing that God will find a way." The boy spoke with rising emotion, and the artist, comforting him, said, "Come, sit here. Your father's faith is strong, my boy. He is right; God will make a way. You spoke in anger about money falling from the sky, but in a sense, it's true because God is up there," he said, laughing at his own joke, and then filled the boy's hands with bundles of money from the bag.

It took a moment for the model to grasp what was happening. "Sir, what are you doing? Please take it back. This is your prize money, hard-earned. I know how much you struggled," he said. The artist reminded him, "Do you not remember, I promised you half of the prize if I won." The model laughed, "Who takes such jokes seriously? But you are different." The artist insisted, "It might be a joke to you, but it was a promise to me. Take it without argument. Use it to pay for your son's education." The boy's face lit up. "Uncle, is this really happening?" he asked. "Yes, my boy. Without a person like your father, I would never have created such a masterpiece," said the artist. The model, overwhelmed by the artist's generosity, held his hands with love and said, "You are like a brother from a previous birth... I am speechless." The worry lines on the model's face began to melt away. The artist watched his face intently, marveling at the transformation, "Seeing your smiling face now, I might have to paint another portrait of Tagore," he said. The model, understanding his intention, replied, "I am ready to sit for as many portraits as you want, even giving up my job," he said, smiling. The artist, finding the humor delightful, laughed heartily, and the model joined in freely. And the young boy, too, shared a heartfelt laugh, relieved that their problem was solved so unexpectedly.

Indeed, Tagore's life was vast and full of infinite faces. The artist had captured just one face.

A Twisted Tale

As the rose petals in her hair, which were shining brightly, began to wither, her dreams of a beautiful life with Varun also started to fade. With each passing moment, the despair grew, and she struggled to hold back the tears welling up in her eyes, telling herself, "He will come now, he will come soon," waiting for him. She had adorned herself beautifully and carefully for him. Her hairstyle was modern, with a rose slightly blooming on one side, and she wore an attractive blue georgette saree with a shining black border. Her jewelry sparkled like stars, and her designer pallu matched perfectly. The lipstick on her soft lips added to her beauty without being too bold. She wore expensive, glittering sandals, hoping that one look from him would captivate him with her charming smile. Whispering "My Varun, my Varun" softly to her heart, she hurried towards him.

But when she arrived, the owner of the renowned software company, who was on the phone when she arrived, looked at her indifferently and said, "Hi" with a raised hand, indicating the waiting room. Being near his chamber, she could hear all his conversations. He was scolding the engineers for not completing the programming on time. Two clients were seated in front of him, and the engineers stood with their heads bowed. He was also attending calls in between. After ten minutes, she looked over to catch his attention again, but he was still engrossed in angrily scolding. After another half hour, she got up in frustration and left. When he noticed her leaving, he signaled with his hand that he would be there in five minutes. Trying to suppress the tears welling up, she pressed a handkerchief to her mouth and ran to her car in the corridor. Opening her purse, she took out the movie tickets she had kept inside, tore them up, and drove home. This was not the first time she had felt disappointed. Only seven or eight times had they managed to go out together.

At five in the evening, he rushed to the waiting room for Kavitha, only to find it empty. Realizing she must have left in anger for making her wait, he felt bad but thought, "Can I leave such important work to roam around with her for movies and parks?" He didn't dwell on it much, as he had been busy with business affairs since morning. Despite having several cups of coffee, he only felt truly refreshed by his mother's hot filter coffee and drove home. His father, a private school teacher, had struggled to put him through engineering. The difficult moments were etched in his memory. Financial hardships had marked his young mind. His father had passed away after marrying off his two daughters and supporting his education. The determination to earn enough money became his driving force. Through hard work and intelligence, his dreams came true. After gaining experience in several prestigious companies, Varun started a significant venture with friends. His father did not live to see his successful days. For thirty years, his mother had been urging him to think about marriage, but he always joked, "My business is my wife," and left. When Varun became wealthy, distant relatives began to draw closer, showing interest in building relationships. Varun had a special affection for his mother's brother, Prahlad Rao, who was not one to beg for money. Varun admired his simplicity and goodness. Prahlad Rao had lovingly raised his motherless daughter Kavitha without any lack. Kavitha, studying computer engineering in her third semester, was beautiful. Varun's mother hoped Varun would marry her. Not wanting to hurt his mother's feelings, he agreed but kept postponing the marriage for two more years, to which his mother angrily replied, "Fine, marry when your hair turns grey."

Although his mother was happy her son was earning well after years of financial struggle, she felt he was overly engrossed in business affairs all the time. Despite Kavitha's efforts to win Varun's affection, she had not succeeded. Frustrated with his neglect, she began seriously questioning if she would be happy marrying him. Seeing him as a machine devoid of emotions like the lifeless computers in his company, Kavitha decided to tell her father that she didn't want this marriage. She felt that while money was essential, it wasn't a solution to all life's problems. She realized Varun was blind to the deeper aspects of life beyond his limited world of wealth.

One day, while Varun's mother and Kavitha's father were discussing wedding arrangements, Kavitha gathered the courage to sit in front of them. Varun's mother affectionately said, "Come, my dear daughter-in-law," drawing her close. Looking at her father, Kavitha said, "Dad, what I am about to say might hurt you, but I have to say it. Please stop all the marriage discussions and preparations." Both of them looked at her in shock. "Kavitha, what are you saying? Where will you find a groom like Varun? Forget these foolish thoughts," her father said. Varun's mother, surprised, asked, "Did Varun say something to you? Did he hurt you?" Kavitha, with sarcasm, replied, "Does your son even have the time to notice or say anything to hurt me? If he had, it wouldn't have been this frustrating.

Besides business, he needs nothing else in this world. Marrying a machine that produces money, that's all it is," she said. Apologizing, she softly held her mother-in-law's hand and left.

Varun's mother was genuinely hurt. She had dreamt of Kavitha as her lovely daughter-in-law, but she had now dismissed her son as a 'money-producing machine.' Despite trying not to, tears welled up in her emotional eyes.

Seeing his sister's tears, Prahlad Rao felt distressed. "Let it go, Pramila. She's still a young girl. What does she understand? She's grown up happily. How can she know how much money is needed for life? Varun and I know," he said. Wiping her eyes, Pramila replied, "I'll leave now. Your daughter says like this," and she left. Prahlad Rao called after her, "Eat before you go. Also, talk to Varun a bit. Ask him to take some time off and go out with her. Doesn't she have desires too?" Pramila responded, "I've said enough already. You talk to him once; I'll go now," and she left without eating. For many days after that, Kavitha didn't step foot in Varun's office, and he didn't worry much about it. Yet, whenever he found a moment to sit and rest, Kavitha's memory would creep in from some corner of his mind. For a brief moment, he would feel the loss of something precious, but it wouldn't last long. A business call was enough to drive away this thought. As usual, he would become the old Varun again.

One day, while driving to the office from home, Varun saw Kavitha sitting in a car with a handsome young man and was taken aback. Noticing his son's happy mood, his mother once again broached the subject of his marriage to Kavitha. "She's a young girl; she must have the desire to go out and enjoy. Don't be so harsh with her..." Varun interrupted, "Mom, why do you worry so much? I don't have time to leave my work and roam around with her. Now she has found some boy to go out with, let her be..." His mother was shocked. Varun continued, "I have no jealousy; let her be happy. Don't bring up the topic of marriage again," and he walked off to his room. After Varun left for the office, Pramila ran to her brother's house. Prahlad Rao consoled his sister, saying, "Pramila, I know about this too. Her father is known to me. The marriage is fixed with that boy. The debt will be settled there. I don't particularly like the boy either. They aren't financially stable. If I tell her, she won't understand. She spends so much that he will have to sit with his head in his hands. I have shown her great love because she is a motherless child. Whatever is written on her forehead... let it happen," and Pramila left without another word. Within a month of this incident, Kavitha's marriage was arranged and took place. Her husband, Pradeep, was a clerk in a bank. A few days later, he was transferred to the Mysore branch and took his wife with him.

As Pramila grew older, health problems began to surface. She suffered from leg pain and back pain and struggled despite medication, pills, and tonics. She longed for a daughter-in-law in the house. Gathering her son, she said, "You see my suffering. I can't cook for you regularly anymore. Won't you listen when I say you should marry?" Her son melted, feeling that if he caused his mother more pain, he wouldn't be human. Despite having a cook, Varun preferred his mother's cooking. "Alright, Mom, let it be as you say. I will marry whoever you approve of," he said, which filled his mother with boundless energy. "Wait, I'll make you some good coffee," she said, rushing to the kitchen. Varun married Shambhavi, the girl his mother approved of, without protest. Once again, he immersed himself in his business empire, working day and night until his health deteriorated to the point where he had to rest at home, which frustrated him. When the new managing director, a dynamic young man named Prashant, assured him, "Sir, don't worry. I'll take care of everything," he felt a bit relieved.

Being homebound, he started interacting properly with his wife, listening to the sound of her bangles, witnessing her selfless care, and seeing the maternal love in her eyes. The saying "A wife is a servant in deeds" proved true. Pramila felt content seeing her daughter-in-law moving around the house with the jingling of bangles. Her health improved under her daughter-in-law's care. In the peaceful home atmosphere, Varun's feelings of affection began to blossom. He found joy in being with his family, his wife, and his mother. Going out with his wife for movies and outings, he realized how beautiful this world is.

A hidden memory of Kavitha would surface in his heart. "Wasn't this what she wanted? What was her fault in that? I troubled her a lot," he would think. When Varun's wife became pregnant, Pramila was overjoyed. After the baby was born, Varun changed even more. This felt like real life. Even when he went to the office, he wasn't as tense. Prashant was a competent worker. Now Varun spent a few peaceful hours at home. Since the arrival of his daughter-in-law, Pramila, who had been active and bustling, fell ill again. When she didn't recover quickly, Varun became worried. Despite taking medications, she grew weaker by the day. When her stomach swelled, Varun admitted her to the hospital. Cancer had silently and stealthily advanced to a stage where it was killing her cells.

Chemotherapy seemed to help a little, but the illness became serious again after a few days. When she couldn't even tolerate liquid food, Varun, desperate, held the doctor's hand and pleaded, "Doctor, save her somehow. I'm ready to spend any amount of money." A lot of money was spent, but his mother didn't survive. Unable to even imagine a world without his mother, Varun was devastated.

For a few days, he was lost in his grief, constantly thinking about his mother. Prahlad Rao, Prashant, and his business friends consoled him, helping him recover to his former self. Although he became himself again thanks to Shambhavi's care, the memory of his mother remained a permanent sorrow in the depths of his heart.

Once, due to work related to his company, Varun had to go to Mysore. After finishing his work, he remembered Kavitha. "I troubled her a lot. When my mother was alive, she used to insist that I see her when I went to Mysore. Years have passed since I last saw her. Mother had said that Kavitha rarely visited her father's house. Once, my brother-in-law mentioned that she was working in a prestigious company. Like you, she has the enthusiasm to start her own business," he had said. This was about five or six years ago. After his mother passed away, Rao had come to Varun's house a couple of times and proudly said that Kavitha now owned a software company.

Varun searched for Kavitha's house address in Mysore. The house was locked. The neighbor said, "Madam is in the office now," and gave him the address. The address was close to the house. It was a tall building touching the sky... with a big signboard saying "Kavitha." Varun was astonished. Climbing the steps and entering inside, he saw her chamber right in front. Kavitha was on the phone talking to someone. When she unexpectedly saw Varun, she was surprised but didn't show it. She raised her hand and pointed towards the waiting room, indicating for him to wait. It felt like a slap on his face. The waiting room was well-furnished. He flipped through the newspapers on the coffee table. Half an hour passed, and there was no sign of Kavitha. When he peeked in, she held up five fingers, indicating five more minutes. For a moment, Varun felt angry but then smiled. By five o'clock, she appeared in the waiting room. Varun said, "Finally, you came." Just then, the coffee arrived. "Varun, I'm sorry I kept you waiting," she said. Though she looked like a mature woman now, she still looked graceful. However, it seemed she was not as interested in adorning herself as she used to be.

Before Varun could say what he had intended, she started speaking. "Varun, my husband is a clerk in a bank. In the intoxication of love, I ignored this. He is so self-respecting that he couldn't tolerate my father giving me money. He would fight about not accepting it. He didn't like me going to my father's house. Realizing I wouldn't be happy marrying you, I married him. Having never faced financial difficulties and spent freely, I felt suffocated here. I gained experience working in a couple of good companies. With courage, I started my own small business, taking my father's help despite Pradeep's objections. Remembering your dedication and diligence, I worked hard and grew it to compete with your company. Look, Varun, nothing matters more than money," she spoke in one breath, finishing everything she wanted to say. Varun listened to her in astonishment. It felt surreal to him. His words remained unspoken. At that moment, her PA came and said, "Madam, Mr. Gopal Sharma from the company has arrived." Kavitha immediately stood up and said, "Oh, I forgot. Look, I was waiting for them. Varun, sorry, we'll meet again," and without waiting for his response, walked briskly to her chamber.

Varun felt, "Is this how human emotions change over time? Situations and necessities change a person's feelings. After a few years, if her experiences change her feelings again, it wouldn't be surprising," and a wise smile crossed his lips. As Varun passed by her chamber, she was so engrossed in her work that she didn't even notice him.

Beauty & Silence

Just as I was leaving for the office, standing at our home's gate, my wife Pallavi voiced her concern in a somewhat annoyed tone"Let's go to the movies today, hurry up or I will definitely not speak to you if you forget again," Her words were literally true. I tend to forget things easily. Sitting at my desk, burying my face in old files, I'd forget everything to the point of headache. "Hey, are you thinking so hard that you even forgot to leave for the office?" she said, and her voice made me attentive, snapping me out of my daze. As per my daily routine, I pulled her close, gave her a kiss on the cheek, and then left for the office.

When I stepped outside, my gaze drifted towards the opposite house. The house that had been wearing a 'To-Let' sign for two years now looked freshly painted. Someone had moved in a couple of days ago, the new tenants. When a beautiful face peeked from the window of that house, my stride halted. Such beauty! Forgetting I was late for the office, I admired the serene beauty of that woman's face. Had there been more time, I might have turned into a poet or an artist, composing poetry, lost in the sea of description.. then the face disappeared from the window. A slight tremor of remembrance of my wife passed through my body, and I looked back. She was not there at the gate anymore. I sighed in relief and turned my gaze to my wristwatch. The word 'cinema' etched by my wife on my forearm brought a smile to my face. "Poor thing! I must not disappoint her today," I thought, heading towards the bus stop, filled again with the thought of that unparalleled beauty. After finishing the mechanical, tasteless office work, as I headed home, my eyes involuntarily searched for that face in the windows or doors of the house across, but to no avail. Disappointed, I reached home where my wife greeted me with a cup of coffee.

The fatigue vanished as I sipped the coffee. "Is this not the nectar of earth?" As I drank, my wife's stern promise echoed. "Look at your forearm, see! Now you remember. My beloved husband forgets me," she said, pointing to where 'cinema' was written, now washed away by water during lunch. I struggled internally on how to appease her, how to resolve this? As I marveled at her beautifully adorned face, tears streamed down her cheeks.Before I could speak, she had already walked into the bedroom. "Where's my queen?" I realized she was upset and had retreated. I followed inside, hoping to ease my anxious heart, preparing myself for her to express her upset feelings. There she was, sobbing softly on the bed in a half-sitting, half-lying posture. "Oh Darling," I whispered, and a scolding followed. "Enough with your words of love. Being with you is like being in a dream, where everything feels unreal. Couldn't even fulfill the wish to watch a movie. You come home having washed away the reminder written on your hand. This isn't forgetfulness; it's intentional. This is my fate, my karma," she lamented. I started to apologize, "Look, instead of offering food to your hungry husband, you prioritize cinema over me! Do you not trust me?" I moved closer, thinking kissing would not work this time. "Promise, I won't forget tomorrow , "If needed, I'll even place a vow at your feet," I said as I moved to touch her feet. when she pushed my hand away and covered my mouth, saying, "No... don't say such things... it makes me feel guilty." I confidently drew her closer and said , "Do you know about Jayadeva's Gita

Govinda? Just like how Krishna appeased an angered Radha with 'Smaragarala Khandanam, mama shirasi mandanam, dehita padapallavam udaram,' placing Radha's feet on his head, even though the poet wished to write it, he hesitated, fearing it might be disrespectful, and stopped the poetry there. But then, Lord Krishna himself, disguised as a poet, went to Jayadeva's house and fulfilled the poet's desire by writing it exactly as the poet wished. What are we in comparison to that?".My wife quipped, "You always charm me with your words, forgetting my wishes more eager to eat a snack as soon as you come from the office than to fulfill your wife's wishes, Bakasura," she teased me playfully before heading inside the kitchen , I thanked, folding my hands towards a calendar of Lord Krishna. "Are you coming to have snacks too? Let's eat together," I called her. As we sat down to eat, she said, "Look, someone has moved into the house across. The wife looks like Goddess Lakshmi herself. And the husband..." she paused and burst into laughter, her eyes welling up with tears from laughing so hard. I gently tapped her forehead, "What's made you laugh so much?" She tried to compose herself but resumed laughing before she could say "husband". At that moment, someone knocked on the door. Stopping her laughter, she went to open it. "Who could it be at this hour?" I wondered, stepping outside with curiosity. A dark, stout man with a mustache stood there. In that dark face, it was hard to discern his features, yet there was a semblance of civility and gentleness. "Sir, my name is Janardhan, and we are the new tenants living in the house across from you. We actually need some water," he said. I stood there, surprised, recognizing him as the owner of 'the face' I had seen. "Do you need drinking water?" my wife inquired.I welcomed him inside, "Come in, don't just stand there!" He entered with reluctance. We talked for a while, and from our conversation, it was evident that despite his unremarkable appearance, he was rich at heart, a truly respectable householder. He took the water and left, saying, "Thanks "." I invited him to bring his family to home once ".

After he departed, I commented, "Despite his appearance, he's truly a kind man." My wife replied, "Indeed, but wait until you see his wife. They're an extraordinary pair, with a story only known to God." I laughed and said, "Having you as my wife, why should I look at anyone else? Would that be right, or even feasible?" She giggled and responded, "Continue your drama dialogues."

One evening when the new neighbor brought his wife and child over, we greeted them warmly. The child bore its mother's beauty. Probably around two and a half years old. I had admired the beauty of 'that face', and today, I witnessed the beauty of the woman in person.It seemed as if Brahma dedicated all his creative energy to this masterpiece, achieving a hundred percent success. The long hair, her stature, the way she walked, her smile, grace, and beauty... as I admired this unblemished beauty, my wife's scrutinizing gaze brought me back. I was captivated by the child's appearance and gestured for it to come over. The child came running with a smile. "What's your name, little thief? Do you talk as much as you steal glances?" I playfully pinched its cheek. The father's face filled with sorrow, and the mother looked down. I wondered, "What did I do wrong?" He said slowly, "God didn't give my son the ability to speak." Just like his mother, he was born mute. My wife was born mute, losing her speech ability at birth. It was passed down from mother to son. After all attempts, I've resigned to fate. " I'm not sure how my wife, who is mute, can become friends with yours or how she will be able to mingle," he said, his voice breaking. "She's shy. We hardly go out. It's depressing to stay in all the time, so I force her out," he shared. His wife's beautiful eyes slowly filled with tears, rolling down her tender cheeks. We stood there, stunned. In such perfect beauty, was there a flaw? Was this the irony of fate? Those beautiful lips, unable to speak? Were they meant only for smiles? Did Saraswati forget to bless Brahma's beautiful creation with speech? These thoughts of compassion welled up, and tears flowed from our eyes....

Mohi-Nirmohi

She had presented him with an unusual challenge: "If you win, I will be yours," she said, bringing her sweet face forward. How could Srujan possibly forget that? She vividly remembers the day she appeared for the position of a bank clerk. When the manager introduced her to the bank staff, her charming appearance immediately captivated him. He had indeed fallen for her at first glance, albeit momentarily. Over time, his true nature was revealed.

Observing a few girls who frequently sought him at the bank, it became apparent: "Oh! He's a thief! Must be cautious. He's a flirt..." Despite this, the recurring glances that haunted and pursued her were inescapable.

Initially, what she mistook for love and devotion quickly dissolved as she saw through the illusion. Even knowing he was a hunter who wooed girls only to discard them later, a certain weakness or natural attraction to his charismatic presence, which seemed capable of conquering not just her but the entire world, made it hard for her to resist his magnetic eyes.

Nevertheless, her wisdom constantly cautioned her, "Beware! Don't fall for it!" Each day at work, the inevitable attraction felt like a torment.

Though she was careful not to fall into his hands, whenever they met, he seized the moment to plead for her love, to be his. She responded with indifferent silence and walked away. Yet, he never ceased his attempts. Such are the lecherous! Like ghosts that cling to one's back...

Professionally a bank employee, she was a writer by passion, and her stories often appeared in popular local magazines. 'Nirmohi', a story which won the 'Best Novel' award, was being serialized in a magazine. She was indeed emotional, but not madly detached from reality; she was aware. Love wasn't everything in life; there were many other aspects necessary for a fulfilling existence. She was among the few intellectuals who aspired for change in the world, in society. She resolved to teach Srujan a lesson and placed an unusual condition before him: he must read all her published and unpublished articles and novels and write honestly about his thoughts on each. Perhaps there were many reasons deep within her for this challenge. Maybe more than just wanting him to turn away from her, she hoped for his transformation, for him to genuinely appreciate her literary world, to love her and her writings, to test whether he would read them or not...

He, inherently lazy and always looking for the easy way out, might have dismissed it as 'an unattainable fantasy' and given up. But it was all an illusion... He took up her books with affection, and when he looked at her with a 'can't live without you' expression, she was deeply moved inside. A friend of him, known to be a pure cheat, often visited the bank. It wasn't hard to guess why Srujan was the way he was from his company. When he accepted the books from her, his friend was there, loudly insisting, "She gave it willingly... this isn't a right you can claim, leave this desire, buddy... you didn't even study properly for the exams before. Now study for the test this lady has set...will you?"

Whenever he came to the bank, she felt as if her entire body was aflame, each time he spoke in vulgar riddles. Srujan was such that whether for good or ill, he was significantly influenced by his company. Magazines were casually flipped as if just for show, as reading wasn't a habit for Srujan, and it felt like a great ordeal to him. But the intense desire to possess her filled him with inspiration. Initially out of indifference and neglect, he began reading, but gradually, he delved deep into the stories. Unknowingly, they drew him in.

Slowly, he found the taste in reading them. Although it was difficult at first to write his thoughts, he eventually got used to it... When he started discussing the characters of the stories with her during breaks, the rest of the staff was surprised. Even she was astonished but soon realized that like he had succumbed to the influence of his wicked friend Nishant, he also succumbed to the impact of the books. One drew him to the abyss, the other lifted him up... Now he didn't just look at her passionately as if to undress her with his eyes, he didn't make mistakes in the Accounts Long Book anymore.

He worked confidently, in a way that made the manager appreciate his work. His attitude towards her became decent and indifferent, which shocked her inner world of love, creating an unnamed turmoil in her heart. An old Hindi melodious song spun in her memory... 'Tune... Kisika Jaan Ko Jaate Huye Dekha Hai, Dekho Mujhse Rooth kar Meri Jaan ja rahi hai' a tumult arose whether she would lose him. Unnecessary anxiety plagued her. The initial seductive glance seemed innocent now. What strange roles of male-female love-premacy!

Vaishali, her close friend, keenly observed her friend's frenzy. She shared everything with her. In 'Nirmohi', the novel's protagonist ultimately becomes a hermit, which was a significant concern for her. Vaishali thought and offered good advice. Use the same weapon that changed him... write a great novel using love as a subject, it will also contribute to the literary world. She found this advice fitting. Thus, her novel 'Mohi' took shape. It gained appreciation from everyone and again won the 'Best Novel' award.

She was on stage during the award ceremony, her eyes and heart eagerly waiting for him. Srujan finally came. Someone called him and seated him in the front row. She was relieved. After the ceremony, when the fans congratulated and left, he returned the 'Mohi' novel to her with a smile and walked away. After she reached home, she opened the book anxiously and found a letter

Hearty Greetings !!
Congratulations !!
'Life isn't about seducing with glances or pursuing fleeting pleasures. Your books have opened my eyes to a vast, delightful world beyond superficial attractions. I've learned that the essence of life lies not in fleeting desires but in meaningful connections and deeper understanding. You are my true friend.' This realization tore apart the lowly desires nestled in his eyes and made 'true companionship' settle there. The myriad faces of love described in the pages of Mohi were a grand vision for your love's deep longing in my heart. This is another feather in the cap of your success in the literary world...'
Forever yours,
Srujan.

Tears, those silent witnesses of her inner tumult, softly fell upon the pages of 'Mohi.' Holding the letter close to her bosom, she felt a surge of tender affection, as words whispered promises of enduring love.

The Golden Illusion!!

The divine favor was revealed through the beauty of nature. As I gazed at the green trees and hills, which seemed to be in motion, I was engrossed in the beauty of nature. My attention was caught not by the view but by the loud voices of the women sitting opposite me. They were enthusiastically discussing their husbands' exploits, occasionally laughing at their follies. From the moment I boarded the bus, their relentless chatter had not ceased.

It had started with sarees, then moved on to gold, and now onto their husbands. One woman noticed me looking and laughed, "Sorry madam, are we bothering you?" Perhaps she saw my gaze shift towards them. Another said, "We two are friends. From the days we wore jumpers to school... hence so much comfort... so much noise." "Oh no, not at all," I had to reply politely. They then got lost in their animated descriptions of their husbands' antics. I turned back to the magazine I was reading, immersing myself in a good story that uplifted my mood, though they had returned to discussing sarees by then.

"Look, that peacock blue saree with golden motifs that I have... you always admire it whenever you see it," one remarked teasingly. "Go on, even when I admire, you never give me anything," she laughed. "You are more important than that saree... if you want it, take it," her friend responded. "Alright, alright, you gave it, I took it, now keep going," she said. "That's the one I kept aside for my nephew's wedding." "And my sky blue saree with the swan on the pallu... that has its own story too," the other added. I turned my gaze back outside. The same sky, the same earth, the same natural beauty... It seemed as if a mystical artist had taken his magical brush and painted everything around. Signs of an approaching village appeared as houses started to become visible sporadically. People were bustling about. When I turned my attention back inside, they were discussing thieves. "Not a single locked house in our area has been spared. With gold prices skyrocketing, the amount of thefts has justifiably increased..." one lamented. Her friend added, "What are you saying... Just the other day, right in front of our house in the morning, while the women were drawing rangoli, someone snatched their mangalsutra..." This conversation made me think about my friend.

A friend who had been insisting that I come over to see her new gold necklace, a long-cherished desire that had finally come true—I beautifully imagined gold necklace, about how many grams it should weigh, its shape, and design all meticulously thought out. "My husband's due salary arrears will come, and he has promised to have it made," she would repeatedly assure over the phone. The necklace would only enhance the beauty of her already radiant smile, I imagined, as I gave in to her insistent demands in a fortunate moment and boarded the bus. My trail of thoughts ended as the bus stopped at a station in some town. A little girl on the bus stretched out her hand asking for something.

After rummaging through my purse, I handed her five rupees; her big eyes and full display of teeth seemed like I had handed her a treasure. A few minutes later, I was introspective again. Thoughts of my friend Hemmi resurfaced. Her husband worked as a clerk in a small private company. Hemmi hadn't brought many jewels from her parental home. Her father had struggled to make a single mangalyam chain, two simple bangles, and small mango-shaped earrings for her ears. Hemmi was worthy of her name—lover of gold! But fate hadn't allowed her desires to be fully realized even at her husband's house.

Even though she was beautiful, her parents couldn't afford a dowry to give her to anything but a simple clerk. She was often angry with them. Always smiling, her complexion was as fair as cream milk. Her laughter was infectious, and she had a way of enlivening the atmosphere wherever she was. We had been together since high school. Whenever she reproached her parents for marrying her off to a poor man, I used to say, "Oh beauty, shouldn't you have avoided ensnaring any boy while at college?" "Oh go away, I'm not so unfortunate," she would retort, puffing her cheeks.

I too would laugh, "Is loving someone a mistake?" Now, Hemmi had two children. The freshness of her beauty was slightly dimmed by poverty. "Even if her husband had the face of a monkey, it would have been better if he were rich," Hemmi would say sometimes in despair. Now saying this seemed normal, seeing your beloved's face every day," she would then cover her mouth and say, "What can I do with that beloved face?" I had joked, "Kiss him," in a teasing tone. Sripathi tried to console Hemmi, wrapping his arms around her neck like a garland, "Look, this garland of arms, why bother about that lifeless gold necklace, can you put a price on this garland of my love?" he would ask while looking into her eyes. She would have pushed his arms away as if tearing them off. "Look, no money, no gold.. always such talks," she would confide to her friend. But now, her heart blossomed like a flower, full of pride and joy. "Sripathi truly is a 'lord of wealth'," she would be giddy with happiness. When she had called me the other day, joyfully I had said, "Now atleast you will kiss Sripathi's beloved face, right?" From the other end, a loving 'Hmm' was heard. If you were in front of me, you would have seen her blushing face, I thought... the bus was passing through a village. The harsh sound of the horn brought me back to reality. Suddenly the driver honked to avoid a bullock cart ahead... I looked towards the ladies on the opposite seat... after discussing so many topics, they seemed tired... the goddess of sleep had pulled them into her embrace... I drifted back into my memories...

What could Hemmi's parents have done? Keeping a beautiful daughter at home is like holding fire in your lap! They stopped her education in the second year of PUC and found a decent boy named Sripathi to tie the knot... reaching Bangalore quickly, I was more eager to see my friend than her necklace. Hemmi was eagerly waiting to show me her necklace... as evening approached, the beauty of the sunset spread across the sky... as I watched, the sun set and darkness enveloped... those on the opposite seat were still drowned in sleep... sleep also pulled me into its bag, and Nidra-devathe gently dragged me in...

Afraid of the sophistication and chaos of the giant city of Bangalore, I got off at the bus stop and caught an auto to my friend's house. As I could see her house from a distance, I was elated but why were people crowded in front of the house? What had happened? I got off the auto and walked towards the house. An undefined fear haunted me. Making my way through the crowd, I stepped inside only to be greeted with tragic news. My friend lay on the floor in the middle of the house, her body bearing several stab wounds. Blood had clotted from the injuries. Around were several policemen, an inspector... "Step back everyone, don't touch anything...don't move any items," they directed. I felt the ground beneath me split open. "Oh God, what has happened here?" My friend's body lay motionless. Tears began to flow from my eyes as I saw Hemmi's condition. "What has happened to her?" I asked one of Hemmi's relatives standing by. They cried out, "Hemmi has left us all behind." Is this true? I was dumbfounded. A deep anguish filled my stomach. "How did this happen?" I stammered.

I looked around. Hemmi's children were crying, clutching their father who stood dazed. The relatives began to explain. "Some stranger must have come asking for water during the time she was alone at home. Nothing is clear. She might have opened the door to get water, and he followed her in, grabbing her necklace and threatening her with a knife. When she resisted, he stabbed her, the poor thing! When she screamed loudly, the neighbors came running. Everyone together caught the thief as he was escaping. The necklace was recovered... but she was gone. The golden girl's life was taken..." they sobbed. Listening to this, my head spun... I felt choked in that atmosphere and couldn't stand there much longer. Several people stood in front of the house. Unbearable words about my friend's unexpected death, despite my protests, assaulted my ears...

An old woman expressed her sorrow with deep emotion: "This is a tragedy that should never have occurred. She was such a kind-hearted woman. What kind of future are we leaving for our daughters? Are these the darkest days?"

However, the crowd's reactions varied, highlighting different perspectives:

One bystander remarked critically, "She was always so focused on acquiring that necklace. It seemed very important to her."

Another responded with a hint of frustration, "What are you implying? That she deserved her fate because she wanted to improve her situation? She constantly asked her husband for the necklace—it was a frequent topic of conversation among the neighbors."

A third person speculated with a tone of blame, "Why did she even open the door? Was showing off her belongings necessary? If she had been more cautious, could this have been avoided?"

Yet another added softly, suggesting another grim possibility, "And maybe... it wasn't just about the necklace. Given her beauty, despite her modest means, she might have been targeted for more than theft."

Overwhelmed by the insensitivity of the remarks, I found myself shouting louder than I intended, driven by a surge of emotion: "Have you no sense of decency? Must you speak every thought that crosses your mind without considering its impact? Where is your humanity?"

My outburst silenced the crowd momentarily. The gravity of my words made them reflect, and the person I had directly addressed looked down, unable to meet my eyes. My harsh tone had startled many, bringing a hushed pause to the chaotic murmurs.

The overwhelming grief of losing my friend consumed me, and I could no longer hold back my tears. As I wept, the realization of my friend's brutal fate and the callousness of the onlookers' comments deeply affected everyone present.

"Wake up," they gently reassured me, patting my shoulder. I was still on the bus, and we had just arrived at the Bangalore station. Realizing nothing had happened to my friend Hemmi, relief washed over me. It's astonishing how vivid a dream can feel until you wake up. Overwhelmed by this realization, joy surged through my heart—Hemmi was waiting for me. "Oh! What was that nightmare all about?" I wondered aloud as I gathered my things and stepped off the bus, smiling gratefully at the two ladies who had comforted me. I instructed the auto driver with Hemmi's address, my mind still puzzling over the dream's intensity. "People who die in dreams live long," I recalled someone saying. I used to dismiss such sayings as mere superstitions, but now, it felt oddly reassuring. As I approached Hemmi's house and saw her standing by the gate, my heart filled with joy. "Hemmi, Hemmi," I called out, running to embrace her. "First, see the gold necklace... see..." she babbled excitedly. Yet, in that moment, none of it mattered; Hemmi, vibrant and alive, was more precious to me than any gold.

The Mysterious Pen Name: A Tale of Love and Loss

I am not a writer. But I am a lover of literature, a connoisseur, and a compassionate person. There isn't a story or novel that I haven't touched, read, and appreciated. I even enjoy reading the stories published in women's monthly magazines. Aren't they stories written by tender-hearted women? One day, while casually flipping through a monthly magazine, a story that I hadn't read caught my eye. Oh! What story is this? It had escaped my notice. How could I have missed you, dear story? I decided to read it immediately and looked at the title, "Dreamy Tales." The title itself was intriguing. Let's see how the story is. I settled comfortably in an armchair, ready to indulge in the story.

The story began humorously but soon took a tragic turn, piquing my interest. The style, the expression of emotions, the narrative skill, and the storyline all captivated me. The style was so enchanting that it drove me crazy. I finished the story and closed the book. Still lost in the story, I hadn't noticed the author's name. Suddenly, I remembered and picked up the magazine again, flipping through the pages. "Aditi" - what a delightful name. But this author was new to me. She must be an emerging writer. I read and reread the story multiple times, and with each reading, Aditi's writing delved deeper into my mind.

Who is 'Aditi'? Is this a pseudonym or her real name? Is it a man or a woman? The mindset of these writers, poets, and storytellers is quite peculiar. If the writer is a woman, the pseudonym is masculine. If it's a man, the pseudonym is feminine. Sometimes people get so enamored with a writer's style and narrative that they dream of meeting a beautiful young woman or a handsome young man, only to find an elderly person or an ordinary-looking individual when they visit the writer.

I thought about all this, yet questions about this new writer persisted in my mind. Who is this new writer? Where is she? How does she look? Why has she captivated and haunted me? Should I call this a weakness? No, my heart did not agree to call it that. Suddenly, a loud knock on the door broke my reverie. I opened my eyes. Aditi had vanished. The magazine lay open on the table. I rubbed my eyes and opened the door. My friend Rajan barged in with a "Hello."

He said, "What kind of bachelor are you, dreaming about some celestial nymph in broad daylight? What a useless nap this is, even with loud knocking you didn't wake up?" I apologized, "Sorry, I was reading a story and fell asleep. What brings you here after four days?" Rajan, ignoring my question, picked up the magazine and glanced at it. "Dreamy Tales," he exclaimed. "What a name! What kind of story is this?"

"Read it; it's excellent. The style and the choice of words are mesmerizing. It's written by someone named Aditi," I said. Rajan responded, "Aditi? Oh, there was a girl named Aditi studying with me in college, four years ago. I didn't know her well, but she was known to be a good writer and a nice girl. She was quite pretty too. But how can we be sure this Aditi is the same? Forget it, why are you so obsessed with her after just one story?"

He laughed, and I replied, "Hey, don't mock me. Do you know her address?" Rajan, in a theatrical gesture, said, "Oh sir, literature lover, that was four years ago. Who knows where she is now? But let's try. What if she's married now?" Before he could finish, I jumped and covered his mouth, saying, "Don't say that!" My voice trembled. Rajan laughed heartily, patting my back, saying, "Such emotion isn't good, Arjun. It only brings sorrow in the end."

I slowly said, "I have read countless stories and novels. I've spent many days and nights in the library, skipping meals, but no writer has ever drawn me to them like this. But Aditi! She feels close to me, familiar." Rajan's eyes welled up as he listened. Noticing this, I asked in surprise, "What's wrong?" Rajan wiped his eyes and said, "Nothing, just a memory. Forget it. Why don't we go out for a walk? That's why I came. This 'Aditiyana' can wait."

I said, "Let me wash my face, make a strong coffee, and I'll be ready in five minutes. Let's visit the library too," and dashed to the bathroom. As I washed my face, Rajan's words echoed, "Why the library now? Will you read another story and look for the author's address? Am I supposed to act as a messenger between you and the authors?" I called out, "Do you think I'm that frivolous, impractical, and weak?"

Rajan mumbled, "Yes, I'm the fool here," which I overheard.

When Aditi's stories began appearing in the magazine every two or three months, I was overjoyed. A serialized novel followed. I carefully cut out and saved each installment. Rajan noticed this and laughed. I would pester Rajan to find Aditi's address. I even wrote to the magazine editors, requesting Aditi's address. Their response came: "We only receive stories under the name Aditi. We know nothing more. The stories are captivating, excellent, and popular with readers, so we publish them. As per her wish, we send her remuneration to an orphanage."

Upon receiving this response, my admiration and respect for Aditi doubled. Oh! What generosity! Such selfless writers are rare, I thought. The more I thought about her, the more beautiful she appeared in my mind. I felt a deep sense of connection with her. What kind of bond is this?

One day, Rajan came to my room and said, "Arjun, I found Aditi's address. Let's go." Overjoyed, I jumped up and kissed his cheeks affectionately. "That's how a friend should be!" I praised him. His silent, indifferent reaction surprised me. "What's wrong with you? Don't you see how happy I am? Why are you behaving like a monk?" I said as I dragged him along.

Finally, I was going to meet the Aditi who had haunted me with her stories all this time. Rajan put me on a bus. We got off at an unknown place. "Where? Where? Where is her house?" I kept asking eagerly, following him. Rajan walked solemnly. I didn't dare to speak, lost in thoughts of Aditi. When Rajan headed towards a cemetery, I panicked.

"What is this, Rajan? Why have you brought me here? Have you gone mad?" I asked. Rajan laughed loudly, "Me? Mad? I'm perfectly fine. I brought you here to cure your madness. You wanted to see Aditi, right? Just follow me." Without another word, I followed him.

Inside the cemetery, an eerie silence prevailed. Rajan stood in front of a grave, tears rolling down his cheeks. After a few moments of silence, he turned to me and said, "Arjun, do you recognize whose grave this is?" A woman's face slowly emerged in my memory. It was Ananya, Rajan's sister, whom I had loved and then abandoned.

Ananya is now dead. What is the connection between Ananya and Aditi? Why did Rajan bring me here?

I turned to Rajan and asked, "Is this Ananya's grave?" Rajan solemnly replied, "Yes, this is Ananya. She became Aditi after you rejected her and took her own life. She captivated you with her stories after her death." I stood there like a statue. What a cruel twist of fate! Could Ananya have become Aditi, reaching my heart through her stories because she once loved me?

But how was this possible? Was Ananya writing stories all along? So beautifully, so secretly? Darkness slowly enveloped the cemetery. Rajan woke me from my stupor. We left the cemetery and went to Rajan's house. He took me to Ananya's room. On the table were neatly arranged manuscripts of stories and novels. I eagerly flipped through them. They were all the stories I had read in the magazine. There were also unpublished stories. All the stories were in Ananya's handwriting.

Rajan said, "You might be surprised. I didn't know Ananya wrote so beautifully. After she committed suicide, I found these manuscripts in her room. In her drawer, I found her diary. Every page of the diary began with your name. Her deep love for you was evident. But in the last fifteen to twenty pages before her death, she poured out her heart's pain. Reading it, you will understand her turmoil, her inner struggle."

He continued, "Arjun, I've been holding back these words for a long time. I have to tell you now. Although you didn't know Ankit well, I did. He was a good friend of mine, just like you. He was known as a good writer. Ananya admired his stories and novels. He used to visit our house occasionally. Just as I was to Ananya, so was Ankit.

His love for her was pure. You misunderstood and thought Ananya loved Ankit, and you rejected her. Ananya was very sensitive and timid. She didn't have the strength to explain everything to you. You didn't have the patience to listen either. Had she been brave enough to speak up, time might have resolved your doubts and brought happiness. Instead, she internalized her pain and took her own life. She couldn't bear the humiliation of your rejection. After discovering her hidden talent, I began sending her stories to magazines under the name 'Aditi.' Each time they were published, I prayed for her soul's peace."

He added, "You loved her once, which is why her feelings transformed into stories and novels, reaching your heart. If she had lived, she would have become a shining star in the literary world, more than just a sister to me or a wife to you. Even in death, she captivated you with her writings."

With these words, I hugged my friend tightly and wept bitterly.

Unspoken

Manvitha, who was getting ready in front of the mirror, lost track of time. She adorned her thick, jet-black braids with a garland of jasmine, pinned it crosswise, applied a light layer of powder to her face, clutched a few books to her chest, slipped on her sandals, and called out to her mother, "Mom, I'm leaving now, it's getting late." She was in a hurry to reach college on time. Her mother, who was busy with kitchen work, said, "Okay, go on. Always in a rush, never eats properly... barely spends two minutes eating before rushing off," she grumbled.

In her haste to reach the gate, Manvitha was startled. Rahul, who had moved into the house behind hers two days ago, was standing there with an intense look in his eyes. He was outside the gate, and she was inside. That gaze made Manvitha shudder. Her mind whispered, "Does this man have no decency? What should I do now? I'm already late for college." Rahul, as if understanding her predicament, stepped aside. Manvitha hurried off towards college, her anger evident in her steps. His gaze frightened her as his face floated back into her memory. "A serious face, a dusky complexion, a shadow of sadness on his face. Large eyes filled with some unknown sorrow, a long nose, a stern face that still seemed to show a hint of gentleness when looked at closely."

When he had moved in, her mother had said, "Manvitha, he's a good boy. He shyly said to me, 'Seeing you reminds me of my mother.'" Manvitha thought to herself, "Mom has such an innocent nature. In a time when friendships can turn poisonous in an instant, she trusts people so easily. How could I decide a person's character just by one look? But that gaze!" Her glance shifted to her watch, and she quickened her pace. "Today, a new lecturer is coming. What will he think if he sees me coming in late on the first day?" she thought as she rushed to college.

"May I come in, sir?" she asked as she stood at the classroom door. The new lecturer, who was writing something on the board, turned slowly to look at the door. "Come in," he said. Manvitha, upon raising her head, was startled for the second time. It was Rahul, the new lecturer! That same gaze! She felt uneasy. Keeping her head down, she quickly walked and sat among her friends. The new lecturer's captivating voice and unique teaching style had charmed everyone. Everything was fine, but why did he keep giving me that look? she wondered. Her friends noticed the glances too, with Sara next to her pinching her thigh and whispering, "The new lecturer's first glance has fallen on you. What's going on?" Manvitha, filled with anger, replied, "He's just a tenant who moved in behind our house. Please, don't make it a big deal. You have a big mouth, just stay quiet."

Her friend laughed, knowing how the world works. Between a man and a woman, people always jump to conclusions, thinking of only one kind of relationship. Relationships like brother-sister, father-daughter rarely come to mind. Manvitha just wanted the period to end. As the lecturer continued teaching, his gaze lingered on her a moment too long. Several curious eyes turned towards her, and she could hear a few knowing giggles. Manvitha was thoroughly confused.

The period ended, and 'Preethi and Party,' as they called themselves, gathered around the new lecturer, bombarding him with unnecessary chatter, trying to learn about his background. When Manvitha came home and was eating her snack, she couldn't resist telling her mother, "Mom, the tenant who moved into the house behind ours is our new lecturer." She tried to say more, but the words stuck in her throat. Her mother, expressing surprise, said, "Really? I didn't know. He just said he was a lecturer, not that he was at your college. That's good. Leave it, he's a decent boy." Hearing her mother repeatedly call him 'decent' irritated Manvitha. "Enough, Mom. Stop calling him decent. You think everything white is milk."

Her mother, sensing her irritation, asked, "Why are you so angry? What did he do to you?" Manvitha, not responding, finished her snack and went to her room to sit and think. His serious demeanor, the way he spoke, his behavior—all seemed respectable. But why did he keep looking at me like that? If this keeps happening, Preethi and Party will make a story out of it. She remembered his face again, "Maybe something bad happened in his life, maybe he's heartbroken... Whatever it is, what does it matter to me?"

The next day, as Rahul was getting ready to leave for college on his scooter, Manvitha, standing at the gate, saw him. That same gaze! She lowered her head and walked past him. He seemed to want to say something, but she ignored him and walked on. Every day, she would see him at the gate, and every day he seemed eager to say something. Once, she thought of confronting him, but something held her back. The unspoken words remained within them.

One day, Rahul was teaching in class, his gaze unintentionally lingering on her. Manvitha found it hard to focus on the lesson, lost in her own thoughts. Suddenly, her train of thought was interrupted. The lecturer asked someone a question, "Rashmi, will you please answer this question?" Manvitha looked at Rashmi, who stood up, but his gaze was on Manvitha. He pointed at her, saying, "You, yes, you." Rashmi, who had stood up, sat back down, embarrassed. Now it was Manvitha's turn to feel embarrassed. "My name is not Rashmi, it's Manvitha," she said softly, looking down. Rahul, regaining his composure, said, "I am sorry, I thought your name was Rashmi. It's alright, sit down."

Manvitha was puzzled. "This lecturer must be half-crazy," she thought to herself. Sara, tugging at Manvitha's braid, whispered, "Why does he act like that around you?" Manvitha, getting annoyed, replied, "Can you speak without tugging my braid or making fun of me? I have the same question."

On a festival day, Manvitha joyfully cooked a festive meal for her friends and sent them off happily. Seeing her daughter in a new saree, her mother sighed deeply. She wanted to see Manvitha married before she passed away. The thought of Rahul came to her mind. "Poor boy, he's a good match for Manvitha. I should slowly find out more." She remembered, "It's a festival today. What will that bachelor do alone? I should send him some festival food."

Calling Manvitha, who was humming a song by the radio, she filled a plate with various dishes she had prepared. "Manvitha, poor Rahul is alone. Take this to him." Manvitha, startled, replied, "I won't go to his house, Mom." Her mother, caressing her, said, "Go, dear, be a good girl." Reluctantly, Manvitha walked to the house behind theirs, her heart pounding. What should she say? She gently pushed the door open, and the sight inside made her uneasy.

Rahul was standing in front of a woman's photo, his eyes closed, tears streaming down his face. His lips were moving, "My sister

Rashmi, you have finally left me. Your lovely face, sweet words, and smile... how can I ever forget? My dear sister, you know, every time I see Manvitha, I remember you. I see you in her. My tears are my offering to you on your birthday!" Manvitha looked at the photo in amazement. "Oh! This girl looks just like me. Her eyes are like mine. So, this is Rashmi?"

The meaning behind Rahul's looks became clear to Manvitha. Tears welled up in her eyes without her realizing it.

Mother Theresa

Shankari, who was rushing home with a bag of fruits in her hand towards the vegetable market, was stopped by a little boy. The action he was engaged in surprised her, melting her heart. In that narrow, congested street, a funeral procession was making its way towards the crematorium. The procession, filled with so many people, was occupying the entire width of the street, causing significant disruption to the smooth flow of vehicles. Four or five people, carrying large pots, were repeatedly pouring water on the corpse. It seemed as though the entire market's floral garlands were on that body. The fresh, new red roses on the lifeless body were gleaming brightly and smiling. One could easily identify many of the people there as political figures by their attire. She overheard someone nearby talking, and the words reached her ears: "MLA Chidanandappa's son seems to have died. He was in love with a girl from a different caste, and her family did not accept it. That's why he hanged himself..." Before she could hear more, she deduced, "Alright, this is a love disappointment case. But, once people enter politics, they often lose much of their emotional sensitivity. After all, he is the MLA's father, not the son! But still, the political atmosphere comes home too... Anyway, what does it matter to me?" Concluding her analysis, she moved on. As the procession moved forward a bit, the little boy was picking up the remains of the flowers on the tar road behind the body. His face was marked by hunger and a pitiful expression. His head, devoid of oil, and his innocent face, adorned with a torn shirt and shorts with white and blue checks, tugged at

Shankari's heart. Using his tiny hands, he picked up as many flowers as he could and stuffed them into his pocket. Unable to hold back, she called him closer. He approached hesitantly, sniffling. She took out five or six bananas from her bag and placed them in his hands. Looking at her with gratitude, he smiled joyfully. She stroked his head, feeling fulfilled, and hurried towards her home. She thought to herself, "If taken care of from time to time, this boy would look cuter than my son." Remembering the cooker with rice and lentils on the gas stove in the kitchen, she quickened her pace.

Her tension increased as she remembered her daughter, always chatting on the internet, and her mischievous son, engrossed in cartoons in front of the TV. The textbooks had not captivated him as much as the cartoon world did. Thinking of the books trapped in his bag, crying silently, made Shankari want to cry too. By the time she wished to curse the inventor of the TV, a few of her favorite serials with family stories had already engrossed her. Audio-visual media like television is undoubtedly influential. However, we fail in creating programs that have a positive impact. Using the internet for chatting can be worthwhile for knowledge development and information gathering, but if used carelessly for cheap entertainment, it becomes disastrous. Scientific progress can be a boon, but if caution is ignored, it can be harmful. But I can't even control my children, she thought, smiling wryly. "I told my daughter yesterday evening to bring vegetables. She should listen to me at least a little. If she is engrossed in computer games and internet chatting, it's all over," she grumbled. Mornings are a stressful time for all housewives until they send their husbands off to the office. It's true that it's like a bad time. There's no time to even breathe. If unexpected guests arrive at that time, it's all over. If you don't pre-plan the previous night for the next day, a housewife's peace is guaranteed to be disrupted. There will be so much tension that if a thief accidentally breaks in, a stressed housewife might angrily say, "Do you have to come now? Don't you know the time? Come slowly later. All the jewelry is kept here and there. Not now, please." Shankari laughed at her exaggerated imagination. Given the stress of work, such a mindset is not surprising. Approaching the house, at the corner turn near the vegetable shop, the friendly shopkeeper said with a sly smile, "Didn't find bananas in our shop, huh?" Shankari looked at her bag. The yellow tips of four or five bananas were peeking out, catching her eye. She pushed them back inside. "Why push them inside now, madam? I already saw them."

"She should have thought about it beforehand... She has to pass by our shop and always notices everything like a hawk," they said. Shankari calmly replied, "Mother, you have X-ray eyes... I haven't written on a bond paper that I will always buy from your shop, have I?" To this, the seasoned shopkeeper, not wanting to lose customers, responded with humor and conciliation, "Oh madam, I was just joking. Don't get angry, please."

As soon as Shankari turned in that direction, the flower seller started pestering her, "Madam, please buy a couple of garlands and make my first sale. You just walk by without even looking." Shankari, irritated, said, "I'm in a hurry, why are you so worried? I bought flowers yesterday and they are still fresh. Will you let me walk on the street or not? No matter how far I go, you keep yelling 'please, please.' Everyone is watching. This is the last time. If you shout again, just watch."

The flower seller, seeing Shankari's angry face, opened her red-stained mouth wide and laughed heartily, saying to the nearby vegetable vendor, "Look at madam's anger. Her face has turned all red with rage." Seeing the two of them laughing together, Shankari's anger boiled even more.

When she got home, it was already a quarter past eight. Her son, who should have been at school by eight, was watching cartoons with abandon, clapping and laughing loudly. Shankari was furious. Noticing the fierce expression on his mother's face, her son got up and ran, saying, "Mom, please don't hit me. I'll quickly put on my uniform."

Her anger subsided instantly, and she hugged him, kissing him affectionately, her face calm like Buddha, and with a victorious smile, she walked towards the kitchen. Her husband, a Rajkumar fan, was humming a song from one of Rajkumar's movies. Despite being told to reduce the flame after the cooker whistled, he hadn't done it. The cooker was still whistling. "What happened? Didn't I tell you to reduce the flame or turn it off? All the rice and lentils might have overcooked... Oh no," she fretted.

Her husband, nonchalantly, as if nothing had happened, said, "Did you? Sorry, dear... I forgot," escaping the situation. "Poor thing! Instead of becoming forgetful at seventy, he has already started now," she muttered angrily. Her son and daughter left for school. Her husband, ready to leave, said, "I'm going now," and reached the door, but then seemed to remember something, turned back, and said, "Come here. You always keep doing some work. At night, you roam around like a nocturnal creature.

"Come to bed at least by midnight. Just give this to me," he says, hugging Shankari, pinching her cheek and kissing her. Shankari, pretending to be annoyed, says, "What if the neighbors are watching? The door is open, leave me," gently pushing her husband away. Now, she is alone at home. The once noisy house is now filled with deep silence. Finding the silence unbearable, she picks up the remote and flips through all the TV channels, but none of them interest her, so she turns it off. "Nothing good at all," she grumbles, heading towards the kitchen, remembering the mess.

To Shankari, there's as much joy and satisfaction in scrubbing a particularly dirty dish until it gleams or cleaning a filthy piece of cloth until it sparkles as there is in worshipping the gods. She sings a song in her own peculiar tune, "Don't go away, mendicant, forgetting this poor woman who has cooked for you. Why do you leave, ascetic?" In this song, the poet Lakshmi Narayan Bhatt has beautifully translated Meera's profound love and devotion for Krishna into Kannada. "Ah!" she thinks, analyzing that there is an inseparable bond that says, "I will reach you even if I burn to ashes."

When the cuckoo, perched in the mango tree in front of the house, sings sweetly in spring, Shankari's heart is drawn to it. Unconsciously, she starts singing, "This heart will rejoice a hundred times if the cuckoo sings once." As she sings, she finishes her work, all her tension melting away. Suddenly, she remembers she has to correct her son's Kannada notes. Shankari's son has a habit of making every letter aspirated, regardless of whether it's necessary.

Since all her kitchen work is done, she enjoys correcting his notes, laughing as she goes. She reads out loud, laughing to herself, "The 'Vanasuma' poem was taken from the 'Nivedana' collection. Even though the jasmine is in the leaf's cover, it shows humility and bears pride..." She opens the science book, thinking, "My son, the aspirate lover!"

The other day, when Shankari's family went to the temple in their car, there was a long queue. Thinking how people are becoming more religious in this scientific age, she stood in line with her family. While waiting, she

saw a group of destitute children hoping for alms and noticed the same little boy from before. Shankari felt a strong urge to go near him, pat his head, and speak to him. Leaving her sandals with him, she said, "Take care of these, child," and saw a flicker of joy on his innocent face, his eyes sparkling.

After the family finished their prayers and bowed to the serene deity inside the temple, they also paid their respects to the recently installed meditation statue on the temple's upper floor. As they came out, their minds felt a sense of blessed relief from all worries. Shankari's husband, without even properly looking at the boy guarding their sandals, carelessly tossed a one-rupee coin into his palm, saying disdainfully, "Hey... take it."

Even after the children wore their sandals and walked towards the car, Shankari stayed back. Unable to control herself, she asked the boy, "Where are your parents, child?" His eyes filled with tears as he shook his head, indicating he had no one. Shankari's heart ached; she felt an overwhelming surge of compassion. "Why does this boy stir my heart so deeply?" she wondered. Just then, her children called out to her. Unable to contain her emotions, she held the boy's hand and led him to their car.

Turning to her husband, Shankari said, "You remember the funeral procession I mentioned while bringing vegetables the other day?

This is the same boy..." Though her throat felt choked and she struggled to speak further, she mustered up her courage and continued, "Poor thing! He's an orphan! Why don't we take him in? He's such a sweet boy," she said, running her fingers through the boy's hair lovingly.

Her husband, greatly astonished, said, "Shankari! What's gotten into you? Have you lost your mind? If we start taking in every orphan we find on the street, we might as well open an orphanage. Come, sit down. Just be a mother to your own children for now, that's enough." At that moment, she felt, 'Even though everyone is here, am I not also an orphan in a way?' Sadness welled up inside her. She thought, 'What can I achieve without the support of my husband and children, even though my heart is full of compassion? What use is my love and sympathy if they don't translate into action?'

As the question of whether she could abandon her husband and children for the sake of this little boy plagued her mind, her eyes filled with tears as she stared blankly at the temple's tower. The long sigh she let out seemed to answer her question. Her husband, displaying a gesture of generosity, placed a fifty-rupee note in her hand, saying, "Give this and come quickly. Don't be so sentimental."

Shankari, suppressing her emotions like a doll, went to give the boy the money, but he refused. She forced it into his pocket, patted his head, and mechanically got into the car. Exhausted from her mental anguish, she leaned back in her seat and let out a deep breath. Her husband was saying something to her, but in her current state of mind, she couldn't comprehend it. Seeing her distraction, he said, "You can't let these things affect you so much, Shankari. You can help one boy, but do you know how many orphaned children there are in this country?" She remained silent. Despite the chatter of her children and her husband driving beside her, she felt alone. She heard her daughter say, "Mom likes Purandara Dasa's songs, play one," commanding her brother.

Soon, the melodious song of Purandara Dasa began playing from the cassette, "Who has anyone in this transient world? Like bubbles on water, relationships are fleeting..."

As they neared home, Shankari returned to reality when her husband said, "Get down, Shankari, quickly." She got out and went inside the house. Life resumed its mechanical routine. The next day, after sending her husband and children to work and school, she sat alone. Her mind wandered back to the boy. She turned on the TV to distract herself and came across a show she had seen a few episodes of. It was a scene set in an orphanage, where a wealthy heroine was speaking to the orphanage supervisor about adopting a child. It struck her as ironic. 'In the story, everything is smooth, but in real life?' she thought.

The show ended. She turned off the TV and headed towards the kitchen.

As she walked, she noticed a picture of Mother Teresa on the wall slightly askew and straightened it...

Programmed Lives

A gentle smile was always on Priya's face. She looked lovely in a sky-blue saree with peacock designs. Her eyes were shining brightly. Rohit asked, "What's making you so happy, Priya? Your face is glowing with so much joy." Priya blushed at his compliment. She said, "Do you know why I am so happy?"

Expecting her to say, "It's you," he teasingly asked, "Who?"

With a pout, she called out, "Hey Sam, my dear Sam, come here!" In a second, Sam was standing in front of her, "I'm here, Madam. What should I do?" She gently touched the robot's rough hands and said, "This Sam is the reason." Rohit puffed his face even more and asked, "Really? Does this poor husband, who paid so much money to bring him here from Japan, not count at all? Robots with artificial intelligence are rare in this country," he faked anger.

She pulled his face gently, kissed him, and said, "Thanks a lot, Rohit. What should I give you in return?" He replied, "Nothing, just keep smiling always." Priya then said, "Sam, make hot coffee for both of us," and Sam, with a unique hand movement, walked away saying, "Okay, Madam."

Watching Sam walk away, Priya clapped her hands and laughed, "Look, Rohit, how funny and cute he walks." Rohit laughed and said, "I feel a bit jealous of Sam. It seems you love him more than me." She laughed too, "Oh, silly, is that even possible? He's a machine! Can he make me as happy as you do? Can he laugh attractively like you?" she comforted him. He just smiled and touched her cheek, "Oh, leave it, Sam is watching us!" he laughed looking at her.

"Not like that, Rohit, tell me truly! Hasn't Sam brought a new light to our home? Before he came, I used to be exhausted by the time I finished house chores and company work. We have changed so many workers because they never came on time, you know it too. Many times, we had to resort to hotel food as I couldn't cook on time. Sam cooks rice, sambar, vegetables, breakfast every day on time, and when I call him, he promptly says 'Ready, Madam'. I place things so that he can easily find them. Now, I feel so relaxed, you know? Sometimes I even think, this cute rascal Sam has made me lazy," she said.

Rohit agreed, "Yes, Priya, even though humans have a lot of comfort, there's also hardship! Today, the luxurious life we are leading is not entirely good. Occasionally, you should cook too, on weekends, let's give Sam a rest. We can program him for that too. We are the ones controlling him, right?" he laughed.

It's been a week since Sam, the advanced robot, arrived at their home. He has an advanced electronic circuit chip inside him. Just like how God has programmed the human brain, this is designed similarly. But that's God's creation, he is the supreme artist, and it's more perfect. This is human-made and has many limitations. But if you think about it, the credit for this should also go to God! Isn't he the one who gave humans the brilliant minds to create such exceptional robots? Isn't he the great one?

As they sipped the hot coffee Sam brought, Rohit said, "We need to control the number of people coming to see our Sam. Everyone loves the way he walks, talks, and works so efficiently. They watch him with wide eyes. Such robots are rarely seen in homes." Priya replied, "Yes, Rohit. Scientists estimate that by 2030, robots will replace 800 million workers." He said, "It's not that easy. To make robots, we need very intelligent workers. Alright, Priya, you said you would work from home today. I have to go, I'm late," and he hurriedly left.

Their life was like a happy boat, floating on the calm waves of the ocean of family life, heading towards a shore of happiness without any major obstacles. Rohit wanted a child, but he thought it was a big responsibility. Priya also loved children, but they had not seriously discussed it. Whenever the topic came up, she would laugh and say, "Mom's health is not that great. If we have a baby, Sam will have to take care of my maternity too," and Rohit would laugh with her saying, "Program him for that too, he'll do it."

They kept postponing it to the next year, but their parents were eagerly waiting to cuddle a grandchild. They would say, "If it's difficult for you, give us the baby; we will take care of it." During such days, a beautiful girl named Anjali joined Rohit's team in his company. Rohit was respected for his shrewdness, way of dealing with people, and his experience. His always-smiling face, tip-top dressing sense, dedication to work, and patient training for newcomers made Anjali like him a lot. Initially, Rohit was reserved, but gradually, unknowingly, he started getting attracted to her. This attraction wasn't just towards her.

Perhaps, two or three decades ago, there might have been mutual dedication, principles, a sense of protecting each other no matter what, and strong-mindedness among lovers. But over time, these have diminished. It's unfortunate that sexual desire has become the center of everything. As humans pursued worldly pleasures, physical attraction and desires have been mistaken for true love. True love comes with sacrifice. If a loved one rejects them, they positively wish for their well-being.

Externally, we appear to have everything, but internally, we have nothing. Compared to Anjali's attractive body, Priya seemed dull to him. Gradually, Anjali started dancing in his mind even when he was with Priya. Noticing Rohit's distraction, Priya asked him several times, but she never got a satisfactory answer. Trusting him completely, she kept such thoughts aside and remained calm. She could never dream that her Rohit could do such a thing. Sometimes, the work pressure in the company was high. Lately, Priya dreamt of having a baby.

All her married friends had children and would joyfully talk about their kids' playful antics. But now, Rohit didn't want to hear about children. Whenever the topic came up, he would get irritated. Even though she felt sad, Priya would respond positively and smile, pushing away all her dissatisfaction. However, deep down, a small thread of doubt had started to form.

One day, Priya's friend Malavika visited her and said she saw Rohit walking around with a beautiful girl, with their arms linked. Priya couldn't believe it. Such betrayal! Could her Rohit really do this? Tears started to well up in her eyes. That evening, she confronted him as soon as he got home. Initially, he denied it, but eventually, he admitted, "I promise I will stop seeing her, Priya. Please forgive me." She melted at his plea.

Even though he made a firm promise to his wife, all those vows would fly out the window when he saw Anjali. Her charm was too strong to resist. Whenever he met Anjali by the lake, where they always met, the evening breeze would gently touch their bodies and minds. "Anjali, what we're doing feels wrong. My relationship with

Priya is falling apart. Please forget me. If needed, I'll transfer to another department," he said slowly.

Hearing this, Anjali burst into tears. "Forget you? That's impossible. I can't live without you, Rohit. I'll commit suicide," she cried. Even though he asked her to understand his situation, deep down, he wanted to comfort her and wipe her tears. He decided he had to find a solution to this. As night fell, they left the place.

Though the house was peaceful for a few days, gradually, their hearts grew apart, like spilled milk. They realized they were becoming distant from each other. Discussions about having a child might have acted as a strong bond between them, but they foolishly avoided it. They only saw it as an additional burden, not realizing the joy and beauty a child could bring to their lives.

Sam, who didn't know what a heart or feelings were, mechanically did his work. Many times, Priya would forget that he was a machine and place her hand on his rough hands, saying, "Sam, look at how people manage their lives," with tears in her eyes. Meanwhile, Rohit started coming home late. Small sparks would arise between them whenever he did. He tried to convince her with various excuses. "Anyway, Sam is always with you," he would say with a forced smile. Even though he tried to hide it, his guilty conscience was clear.

One day, Sam was in the kitchen. Rohit left in a hurry, saying he had a lot of work and didn't even wait for breakfast. Priya, feeling unwell, said, "I'll work from home today, Rohit." She sat with her laptop and didn't get up. She called out, "Sam, bring me some snacks." "Okay, coming, Madam," replied Sam.

Just then, her phone rang. It was her friend. She picked it up and said, "Hello, Malavika. What's up?" Malavika replied, "I have something secret to tell you. Is anyone around you?" "No, there's no one. Why do you sound so worried?" asked Priya. "Listen carefully, Priya. Your life is in danger this evening. Your husband has programmed Sam to kill you. There isn't much time. Quickly deactivate Sam and check his chip. I got this information from a close friend who works in Rohit's department. Come on, hurry..." Malavika hung up.

Priya sat still, shocked, for two minutes. She couldn't think straight. Then, she regained her composure and decided to act. With tears in her eyes, she thought, "Could Rohit really do this?" She called Sam over and started debugging him. "Oh my God! He has programmed to kill me at 5 PM!" she exclaimed. She quickly changed the passcode. Anger surged through her. She thought about erasing the program and making Sam kill Rohit instead, but her loving nature stopped her. She restored the chip to make sure Sam wouldn't harm her and stood up. She decided there was no point in staying there anymore. The world was vast, and she was educated. She could live anywhere. She didn't want to see Rohit's face again. Should she file a police complaint? Would another cruel act solve this evil deed? No, her heart still loved him, despite everything. She wrote a letter, kissed Sam's hands, took what she needed, and left.

On the other side, Rohit was floating in a sea of happiness, thinking Sam would have finished the job by now. Somewhere deep down, a small fear was lingering, but he brushed it aside in his lust. "I became very cruel," he heard someone shout, but it felt like it came from far away. He dismissed it, thinking it didn't matter now. He would never leave Anjali. He walked in with some nervousness. Everything seemed calm. He thought his plan had worked. He searched the house for his lifeless wife, but she was nowhere to be found. He saw a letter on the table.

"Oh, forgive me, girl. Damn it, everything went wrong. I should have changed the passcode," he muttered and picked up the letter. What if she had reprogrammed Sam to kill him? He shuddered at the thought. "She would have done that," he thought, looking at Sam. Sam stood still, emotionless, as if no one else existed. Holding his rapidly beating heart, Rohit started reading the letter:

Dear Rohit,

I am still alive by God's grace. Shame on your inhumanity and the immoral desire that drove you to this act! If I were heartless like you, I could have reprogrammed Sam to kill you, couldn't I? I doubt if it's Sam who is heartless or you. I'm not running away because you want to kill me; I'm leaving because I don't want to see your cruel face anymore. Despite everything, you have given me love and sweet moments in the past. Those memories are enough for the rest of my life. Goodbye,

Priya

Tears had smudged the last few words. Her words pierced his heart. He sat down in shock. "Oh God! What a treasure of love I lost, what a fool I am," he said, holding his head. "My dear Priya, I didn't recognize your loving heart," his heart cried out. The pure love of the heart is eternal and immortal, more than the perishable beauty of the body, he realized.

But now, nothing could be changed. "Anjali," the meteor that crashed into the sky of their love, had destroyed the harmony of their household.

Silent Sacrifices

As Sahana looked at herself in the mirror, she thought about how her face, which had retained the glow of youth fifteen or twenty years ago, now looked so mature. Just the other day, she had been looking at a couple of photos from an old album and laughing for a long time, wondering, "Was that really me?" She realized how much joy it brings to see and laugh at one's old images. The innocent, tender face she saw in those photos had changed so much now. Had the unexpected events of life left their mark on both body and mind? She wasn't a doll that could remain unchanged forever. The sensitive human mind and body, made of flesh and blood, couldn't help but be affected by pain. "Don't dwell on old memories; they are like hungry ghosts that will consume you if you let them," her wisdom warned her.

Sahana was getting ready to participate in a literary event. As she continued to look at her reflection, a saying by Kailasam came to mind: "The only lifelong passion possible is to fall in love with one's own self." Remembering her friends' compliments, "You look great!" she thought, "Yes, at this age, that's enough!" and began to comb her hair. After finishing her makeup, some white hairs started to shine through, reminding her of her age. She laughed at herself, half in sorrow and half in indifference. When two white hairs at the front teased her and evaded her grasp, she carefully plucked them out. She hid the rest among her black hair and used a pencil to touch up where needed. The dimples that once added charm to her round cheeks now joined nearby wrinkles, mocking her efforts. Despite her attempts to hide the wrinkles with makeup, she couldn't completely succeed. After finishing everything, she pinned a white rose to her hair, thinking, "Even maturity has its own beauty," and stepped out, feeling satisfied. If no one else appreciates you, you must appreciate yourself, or life will become meaningless, right? That's probably why Kailasam said so.

The memory of her lost youth still haunted her. Were those days of energy and enthusiasm really gone? During that period, she had faced one disappointment after another, becoming a silent statue of despair, drained of enthusiasm. "Oh, I should have made more meaningful use of those days!" she sighed. But, time moved on, leaving behind memories that pierced her heart, saying goodbye and slipping away. Sahana shivered. Just like Vikram being haunted by Betaal, memories clung to her, drawing her into a maze of recollections. The moment she stepped into her husband's house after marriage wasn't as honored as it should have been. Within a few hours, her keen eyes and mind grasped the behavior of her in-laws, their rough manners, and the culture of her husband's family. Their harsh behavior and sarcastic remarks wounded her innocent heart. She wondered, "Why is it like this?" It dawned on her that life here wouldn't be as smooth as a sliding rock.

She soon realized her husband's nature of not making decisions for himself. This made it easy for his family to use him for their selfish purposes. She felt she had missed the mark in choosing her life partner. But all the selection processes were over, and the grand wedding ceremony had been completed. Her chance was gone. She lacked the courage to leave. Seeing the cruel ways society was changing, she knew that leaving her husband would be like "jumping from the frying pan into the fire." She couldn't bear to hurt her parents and didn't want to become fodder for society's poisonous tongues. Holding on to the hope that things would get better in the future, she cast her line, waiting for the fish of hope. She kept her laughter and tears close together.

However, her husband's family had a tight grip on him, like a vise. She had to endure sorrow for even the smallest matters in the coming days. The people around her were famous examples of pettiness and meanness. Despite the values instilled in her by her parents, she tried to treat them with love. But the blows from her husband's harsh behavior left permanent scars on her heart. Watching beautiful marital scenes in movies, she would blush and dream of a sweet life, only to see her castles of dreams crash down.

When her husband first got a small job, his income was always awaited by many mouths. Small matters were exaggerated, and Sahana's husband's ears were filled with complaints, their seeds of intolerance working well in his mind. Fearful of unexpected abuses, Sahana shrank like a frightened sparrow. She thought she wouldn't survive if she stayed with them for long. Perhaps some god heard her prayers, as her husband got a better job in the city. Now, she could breathe a bit easier. However, her desires for food, clothing, and outings had faded, hidden behind a curtain of indifference.

Now, her husband had a high-paying job, and their children had grown up and flown abroad. People in the town eyed her husband's large salary, always finding some excuse to borrow money, sending shameful and insulting messages from far away, always with their hands outstretched. There was a guarantee that some thousands would always fall into their pockets, so laziness had also taken over their shoulders. Sahana thought, "We are living as if we are dead! Is there no value for our existence? Should we keep our opinions to ourselves and suffer?"

One day, she decided to make her husband aware of this issue. She tried to explain, "Is there no end to this thirst? Even after generously responding to the needs of his siblings, helping improve their living standards and financial status, their begging hands continue to stretch further." But as soon as she brought this up, her husband reacted like a volcano, spewing lava. Later, he became silent and stopped talking altogether. The house was engulfed in a cemetery-like silence for two or three days, which was unbearable for her.

In the past, she had become accustomed to making sacrifices for the happiness of the family. She noticed that her husband had been waking up three or four times in the middle of the night and couldn't sleep properly for two days. She, too, wasn't sleeping well. Sleeplessness had become her close companion since their marriage. She blamed herself, thinking that talking about money had caused her husband's sleeplessness. After all, she was an Indian woman, wasn't she? Her husband slept late in the morning, and daily routines were getting delayed, causing trouble.

"Why should I worry, having spent three-quarters of my life? Let him be happy, even if it means giving something away. What's the point of anything, anyway? Can we take anything with us?" she thought, firming her resolve. But the old memories burned her chest. The more she suppressed them, the more they resurfaced. She recalled the many nights she had cried herself to sleep, feeling abandoned and alone, without a single word of comfort. These memories made her clutch her chest in agitation. "Never mind, men are like that!" she thought, trying to push the memories away. "What else can a woman do but endure?"

Determined, she decided to welcome her husband with tasty kesaribath, upma, and good tea. She chased away her laziness and quickly went to the kitchen. Soon, the aroma of the snacks filled the house. She washed her face, dressed nicely, adorned herself with a rose in her hair, and got ready. Just then, the doorbell rang! She ran and opened the door. But it wasn't her husband; it was his brother and his sister's children. She was surprised. Seeing their faces brought a rush of bitter memories, making her anxious. But she quickly composed herself and welcomed them.

The hot kesaribath and upma were ready with their names on them. They thought it was great timing, enjoyed the snacks and tea, and felt it was a good omen for their visit. They waited for Sahana's husband. Behind their excessive politeness, fake smiles, and artificial sweet words, she sensed their intentions to ask for money. She felt strange emotions as she watched their hands, which seemed to grow longer, spreading out like a web to cover the entire house. When their hands seemed to stretch towards her from the kitchen, she screamed loudly in fear.

"What happened, sister-in-law?" asked the children, rushing to her. She brought her mind back to reality and tried to calm herself, saying, "It's nothing. I just felt a bit dizzy." She then thought, "What kind of illusion is this?" Just then, her husband arrived. She sighed in relief. Seeing everyone, he joyfully sat down to talk to them. She brought him the little bit of kesaribath and upma that was left at the bottom of the dish.

"Did you give them snacks and tea?" he asked her. They answered for her, "We've had everything, you go ahead." After drinking tea, they quietly began to ask for money. She understood it was a plea for money. She watched helplessly as her husband took out 50,000 rupees, which she had saved for special occasions, from the cupboard and handed it to them. She couldn't breathe, feeling an indescribable pain. She thought they would never leave them alone until they had drained them completely. Tears of helplessness rolled down her cheeks. She didn't say anything about her decision after they left. What would be the point? What could she do?

That night, she saw her husband sleeping contentedly and a detached smile crossed her lips.

Fateful Meeting

Many times in life, experiences arise that, whether sweet and entertaining or sometimes painfully harsh, become the foundation for great stories. Eager for such unique and strange experiences, I never turn my back on them. I choose a spot in beautiful gardens where flowers fall from trees, creating a carpet of blooms. Sometimes, I find what I'm looking for, but often, I don't. When that happens, I settle for a place where the breeze is cool, sitting on a bench with my trusted pen and notebook. In my small bag, I carry a bottle of water, sometimes an apple or some biscuits. I also carry a phone, but not to make or attend calls, rather to capture the scenic beauty with my camera.

One day, blue flowers were falling from a tree, creating a beautiful sight. A nearby bench was convenient for me. I hurried over, fearing someone might snatch this treasure. Not far from where I sat, there was another bench. After enjoying the gentle breeze for about ten minutes, a young man, seemingly tired from a long journey, came and placed his luggage on the bench, then sat down. He looked worn out, with a mix of exhaustion and despair on his face. After a few minutes of looking around, he glanced at me and asked, "Sir, could you please give me some water?" I handed him the bottle and also offered an apple, saying, "Take this." He replied, "Just water is enough." I insisted, "Please don't refuse. You look like you haven't eaten." He reluctantly accepted and thanked me, then returned to his bench.

He began speaking warmly, "A friend was supposed to come and pick me up, but he's stuck in traffic somewhere. After getting out of the railway station and seeing the dust everywhere, I came here to this garden." I asked, "Is there any urgent work you have here?" He hesitated for a moment before replying, "If I tell you why I came, you might laugh. My parents are forcing me to get married. The girls they are showing me don't interest me. They are getting frustrated, and my mother is so angry she stopped talking to me. I left home saying I would find someone myself. My dear friend lives here, so I came to see if my hope would bear fruit here." I tried to cheer him up, saying, "Good things happen when the time is right."

I then immersed myself in a book. Maybe seven or eight minutes passed. I noticed a young woman approaching from a distance. Seeing her coming towards him, the young man became curious. As she approached, his excitement grew. She sat next to him. He was sweating profusely, not just from the heat, but because she was beautiful, with an innocent, pure, and radiant face. Watching her, the dark clouds of despair in his eyes began to melt away.

The young man, surprised and perhaps thinking his friend sent her, started talking to her. Blushing, she looked down. It's not often a woman so boldly sits next to a stranger without any suspicion. The young man, lost in her pure face, finally asked, "Who are you? Did you come alone? Is no one with you?" She glanced up briefly and said, "They will come soon," and smiled. That smile enhanced her face's beauty. They soon got engrossed in their conversation.

Feeling the heat, I noticed the breeze wasn't as cool as before, and the sun's rays started piercing through the tree leaves. Yet curiosity held me there. The couple seemed lost in their silent conversation, eyes talking more than words. Love seemed to be blooming, and the young man appeared to forget his troubles, lost in the moment.

Maybe five minutes passed. Suddenly, four people, including a woman, came rushing towards them. Surrounding the couple, one shouted, "Here she is. Catch her before she escapes again!" The young man, stunned, stood up to protect her, "Who are you all? Why are you holding her?" I watched in shock and worry. The girl clung to the young man, pleading, "Please don't let them take me, please." The young man, weaving dreams of a new life, was now facing this unexpected misfortune. I shouted, "Hey, who are you all? What did this girl do to you?" One of them replied, "She is mentally ill, we are from the psychiatric hospital. She runs away, troubling everyone by saying she wants a good husband all day long."

Not believing their words, I insisted, "Where is your uniform? Are you trying to kidnap this girl? She can't be mentally ill if she's dressed up like this, and she couldn't have escaped from a hospital in such condition. Should I call the police?"

One elderly man, seeming respectable, showed his ID card, "Yes, sir, your doubt is valid. She found a mother in the hospital who adorns her like this. This is the ninth time she has escaped. We are tired of searching for her." He instructed the others, "Hold her tightly," and they dragged her away. The young man sat on the bench, dejected. "Oh, my fate!" he sighed. He then laughed nervously, "Thankfully, I was saved from that crazy situation." But I couldn't laugh. I pondered on the society that turned such a girl mentally ill.

Just then, his friend arrived, apologizing for the delay. "If you'd been any later, I might have had to admit myself to a psychiatric hospital," the young man joked. He told his friend, "This gentleman saved my life with water and an apple." They both thanked me and left, waving goodbye. I, with heavy steps, headed home, the innocent face of that girl lingering in my memory, tears of sorrow welling up in my eyes.